Consuela spoke, but Slocum was hardly listening. Some silent communication passed between the two that made words meaningless.

"I know what you are thinking, John Slocum," she said, stepping closer.

"I doubt you do," he said. He saw how Consuela tipped her head back slightly. Her red lips parted as her eyes closed. He kissed her hard and she kissed back with equal passion. They clung to each other until they lost their balance and crashed against the brick wall of a bakery. The bricks were warm behind Slocum's back, and he heard the sound of men working inside to bake bread for the morning. The sweet smells of the bread mingled with the taste of Consuela's lips and the warm, urgent feel of her body against his.

She pressed closer to him. His hand moved downward until he cupped her firm buttocks and began to squeeze slowly, sensuously. She moaned and moved even closer until her taut breasts flattened against his chest.

"I was wrong," he said. "You did know what I was thinking."

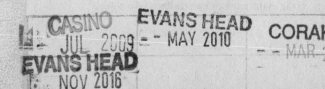

DON'T MISS THESE
ALL-ACTION WESTERN SERIES
FROM THE BERKLEY PUBLISHING GROUP

THE GUNSMITH by J. R. Roberts

Clint Adams was a legend among lawmen, outlaws, and ladies. They called him . . . the Gunsmith.

LONGARM by Tabor Evans

The popular long-running series about Deputy U.S. Marshal Custis Long—his life, his loves, his fight for justice.

SLOCUM by Jake Logan

Today's longest-running action Western. John Slocum rides a deadly trail of hot blood and cold steel.

BUSHWHACKERS by B. J. Lanagan

An action-packed series by the creators of Longarm! The rousing adventures of the most brutal gang of cutthroats ever assembled—Quantrill's Raiders.

DIAMONDBACK by Guy Brewer

Dex Yancey is Diamondback, a Southern gentleman turned con man when his brother cheats him out of the family fortune. Ladies love him. Gamblers hate him. But nobody pulls one over on Dex . . .

WILDGUN by Jack Hanson

The blazing adventures of mountain man Will Barlow—from the creators of Longarm!

TEXAS TRACKER by Tom Calhoun

J. T. Law: the most relentless—and dangerous—manhunter in all Texas. Where sheriffs and posses fail, he's the best man to bring in the most vicious outlaws—for a price.

JAKE LOGAN

SLOCUM AND EL LOCO

J

JOVE BOOKS, NEW YORK

THE BERKLEY PUBLISHING GROUP
Published by the Penguin Group
Penguin Group (USA) Inc.
375 Hudson Street, New York, New York 10014, USA
Penguin Group (Canada), 90 Eglinton Avenue East, Suite 700, Toronto, Ontario M4P 2Y3, Canada
(a division of Pearson Penguin Canada Inc.)
Penguin Books Ltd., 80 Strand, London WC2R 0RL, England
Penguin Group Ireland, 25 St. Stephen's Green, Dublin 2, Ireland (a division of Penguin Books Ltd.)
Penguin Group (Australia), 250 Camberwell Road, Camberwell, Victoria 3124, Australia
(a division of Pearson Australia Group Pty. Ltd.)
Penguin Books India Pvt. Ltd., 11 Community Centre, Panchsheel Park, New Delhi—110 017, India
Penguin Group (NZ), 67 Apollo Drive, Rosedale, North Shore 0632, New Zealand
(a division of Pearson New Zealand Ltd.)
Penguin Books (South Africa) (Pty.) Ltd., 24 Sturdee Avenue, Rosebank, Johannesburg 2196,
South Africa

Penguin Books Ltd., Registered Offices: 80 Strand, London WC2R 0RL, England

This is a work of fiction. Names, characters, places, and incidents either are the product of the author's imagination or are used fictitiously, and any resemblance to actual persons, living or dead, business establishments, events, or locales is entirely coincidental.

SLOCUM AND EL LOCO

A Jove Book / published by arrangement with the author

PRINTING HISTORY
Jove edition / February 2009

ISBN: 978-0-515-14584-7

JOVE®
Jove Books are published by The Berkley Publishing Group,
a division of Penguin Group (USA) Inc.
375 Hudson Street, New York, New York 10014.
JOVE® is a registered trademark of Penguin Group (USA) Inc.
The "J" design is a trademark of Penguin Group (USA) Inc.

PRINTED IN THE UNITED STATES OF AMERICA

10 9 8 7 6 5 4 3 2 1

1

The fierce late morning West Texas sun baked John Slocum's back as he rode toward the Rio Grande River. He had no idea how far it lay ahead of him, but the idea of rapidly running water, abundant water, cool, clear water, drew him like a magnet. He had been out in this godforsaken desert longer than he cared to remember after leaving the Texas hill country, and the heat had started to affect his senses. Mirages were one thing. He watched the silvery heat haze on the horizon and knew it for what it was. But visions were something else entirely. Worse, he heard noises where none should be.

Hallucinating sight and sound meant he needed water as bad as any man ever had, and he was running so low that his canteen sloshed ominously. If he had two swigs left, it would come as a pleasant surprise.

"I need to find some shade and rest till sundown," he said to his mare. The horse turned her head back and glared at him. "All right, *we* need to find shade. And water. Especially water."

Slocum knew there were small watering holes scattered throughout this part of Texas, but he had no idea how to find them. The Apaches learned their whereabouts from the time they were old enough to ride. Slocum needed a map to find those oases, and he didn't have one. He had left San Antonio with the intention of going to Franklin up north and from there into New Mexico until he found cooler country. Taos was high in the mountains and promised respite from the grinding heat that pulled sweat from every pore and beat him down as he rode.

He jerked around, hand flashing to the ebony handle of his Colt Navy slung in a cross-draw holster, when he thought he heard something like paper being scraped over sand behind him. Squinting, he tried to find the source of the sound. All he saw was mesquite, creosote brush, thick clumps of prickly pear cactus, and a whole lot of empty. Even the wind had decided to take a siesta, robbing him of even that small cooling.

Something warned him not to immediately turn back toward the river. His best guess was another three hours' slow walk before he found the elusive Rio Grande, but the chance existed he would not make it at all. Thirst was one thing. Jumping at shadows was another.

He wheeled his horse around to double back on his trail. The hoofprints had already faded in the soft ochre sand, in spite of the lack of wind. In another few hours, there would be no trace that he had ridden this way. That appealed to Slocum in ways he could not explain. He rode without leaving a trail and that was how he wanted to live his life. If he stayed too long in any one place, he might put down roots and come to regret it. With the horizon always his destination, he avoided the worst that life had to offer. In spite of this, he had seen more than his share of misery and death.

The Colt slid from his holster when he heard the sound again. From the corner of his eye he caught sight of movement. He swung his six-gun around and fired. The response came instantly. Three rifle shots, from three different rifles and directions, drove hot lead into his mare's chest and flank. The animal let out a gusty sigh and sank straight down. Slocum kicked free of his stirrups and kept from being pinned as the horse gave one last convulsive kick with her back legs and died.

He dropped to his belly and tried to find even one of the snipers that had robbed him of his horse. During the war he had been a sniper for the Confederacy and had learned one virtue above all others. His patience finally paid off when a swarthy Apache brave foolishly poked his head up to see how accurate his marksmanship had been. Slocum fired three times. One of his slugs caught the Apache in the temple, killing him instantly.

This brought a fusillade that forced Slocum to scuttle backward in search of better cover than the simple rise where he had lain in wait. As he worked his way down into an arroyo, he reloaded. There wasn't any way he would survive a fight with an Apache war party, but he intended to take out a few more before they finally killed him. In the arroyo he looked left and right, then chose a direction at random. His long-legged stride took him a hundred yards down the gravelly, dry riverbed to a spot where he hoped he could get a shot at an Apache lying in wait.

Chancing a quick look over the arroyo rim almost got him killed. The Indians were too wily for such a simple maneuver to fool them. A bullet ripped off his Stetson and sent it flying. He ducked down and waited again. This tactic had worked for him before. It did again. Almost five minutes passed before the Apache came to the edge of the arroyo to see if he had killed his victim.

Slocum did the killing instead. The Apache brave fell heavily. Slocum grabbed the battered rifle dropped by his dead foe and went hunting. He scrambled up the arroyo bank and began wiggling through the thorn-laden sand. After only a few yards of this torture he got his chance. Three more braves crouched together, arguing. He pulled the rifle trigger and had it fall on a dud round. Slocum levered in another cartridge, only to have the same thing happen. A third round jammed in the receiver.

By now the braves had heard the metallic click and thud of a hammer falling on a punk round. All three popped up like prairie dogs, spotted him, stood, and started to fire. Slocum was exposed and in too vulnerable a spot to remain here. He threw away the worthless rifle and rolled, trying to get his six-shooter out and pointed in the Apaches' direction. Three reports echoed across the desert. Then three more. Then a dozen. And silence.

Not a single round had come his direction. Slocum finally got his six-gun out and aimed, but he saw only corpses. The Indians sprawled gracelessly on the ground.

"Don't go movin' 'bout now, mister," came a voice so thick with a Southern drawl that it took Slocum back to his childhood in Georgia. "You know if'n any other of them varmints are round heah?"

"I shot a couple others," Slocum said. He holstered his pistol and looked up at a cavalry sergeant, his dark face beaded with sweat and his wool uniform plastered to his body. The buffalo soldier rode over to him, gave him a once-over, then raised his arm and signaled. A dozen more black soldiers appeared, three on foot and the rest mounted.

"We been chasin' them for nigh on a week. They's part of Nana's band."

Slocum had heard that Victorio had left the reservation in Arizona and sent his band of Warm Springs Apaches rampaging throughout New Mexico and even down into Texas, but he had not realized they had come this far south.

"Nana's one of Victorio's wiliest chiefs," the sergeant went on. He never looked at Slocum. His dark eyes roamed the desert constantly, hunting for more of the renegades. His squad slowly congregated, more to stare at Slocum than to hunt for the Apaches.

"Heard tell of him," Slocum allowed. "An old chief."

"Him and Victorio's sister make quite a pair. Both of 'em are witchy," the sergeant said. "You need to get on outta heah."

"They shot my horse out from under me," Slocum said.

"Then you'd best get to walkin'." The sergeant swung his carbine around and pointed northward. "There's a town not two miles off. If you keep a decent pace, you can make it to Eagle Pass by sundown."

Slocum canted his head and looked at the sky where the sun was just now at zenith. Either the soldier thought he was a slow walker, or he knew something Slocum didn't. Slocum asked.

"In this heat, a man's not going to make half a mile an hour," the sergeant said. "If you wait for dusk, you might make better time, but the desert, well, sir, she cools off mighty fast and you'll have your pearly white teeth clackin' together. Up to you which way you want to endure it. Hot or cold."

Slocum listened with half an ear. The sergeant never once mentioned the possibility of Slocum getting a ride into Eagle Pass with one of the soldiers, which meant the offer was not going to be made. The soldiers were hot on the trail of the renegades and couldn't spare even one mounted soldier to nursemaid a civilian to safety.

"Don't have much water," Slocum said, remembering the telltale slosh in his canteen.

"We just got some at a watering hole not five miles off. Jenks, you give this heah gent your canteen. You can share with Wash and Lemuel." Forestalling a complaint from Jenks, the sergeant said loudly, "You won't catch no cooties from them. Now *they* got some worry 'bout catchin' 'em from *you*, I know."

Slocum appreciated the way the sergeant handled the matter. Water meant life or death, and he had his men chuckling. One buffalo soldier rode over and handed Slocum his battered army-issue canteen. From the weight, Slocum knew it was full. Hiking in the noonday sun might just require him to drink every drop and still be wanting.

"Much obliged. I'll hang on to this and get it back to you," he promised.

"Just don't be gettin' yerse'f shot up by Apaches," the sergeant said. He formed up his squad, and they trotted off in search of the trail left by the Indians, intending to backtrack and find a larger group.

Slocum slung the canteen over his shoulder, then returned to where his horse had been killed. He got the saddle and tack off, slung it over his back, got his bearings, and started walking. It was even hotter than he expected, and the sergeant had pegged his speed well.

Eagle Pass looked like any other dusty town along the Mexico-Texas border that Slocum had ever seen. His feet felt as if he had plunged them into coals, and his back was bowed from the weight of the saddle. Not for the first time, he appreciated how much a horse had to put up with, having a rider and all his gear astride.

He dropped his saddle at the front door to the Hijinx Saloon and Drinking Emporium, dusted himself off, and then went inside. It was almost as hot inside the saloon as it was out, but the promise of a cold beer made it possible to ignore the discomfort and stench. Something must have died in the back room and never been cleaned up.

"You got the look of a thirsty travelin' man," the barkeep said. "You want a bottle?"

Slocum considered getting some whiskey, then shook his head.

"Beer. As cold as you can get it."

"Comin' right up. That'll be a nickel," the barkeep said, hanging on to the handle of the mug before passing it over. Slocum dropped a dime on the counter.

"I'll be having a second one," he said. The coin disappeared as if by magic and the bartender had a second mug of cool beer waiting before Slocum could drain the first and set it on the counter. "I like a place that caters to its customers," he said, grinning. The beer went down cool and made him almost forget the long trek across the desert.

"Hey, mister, you want to set in on a game?"

Slocum turned around and propped his elbows on the bar. Three men at a card table on the far side of the narrow saloon looked at him expectantly. He sized them up quick as a rabbit being looked over by a hungry coyote. Two of them would lose every cent they had on the table in front of them, but the man who had called out was likely to be a professional gambler. He didn't dress like one, but that didn't mean a whole lot in a piss-pit like Eagle Pass.

"I've got a dollar or two," Slocum said. "Reckon I'll take you up on that kind invitation." He got another beer before dropping into the empty chair. He played cautiously for half a dozen hands and saw that he had sized the men up well. The two cowboys played with reckless abandon, folding hands they might win with and bluffing outrageously when there was no point. They wanted the thrill of maybe winning a big pile rather than picking up a dollar or two in a pot.

Slocum and the gambler slowly sucked away the two men's stakes a few nickels at a time. The cowboys finally called it quits after each lost about ten dollars. Slocum faced the gambler, who shook his head in response to the unasked question.

"No, sir. I'm good enough for this town, but I'm not good enough to win against you," he said. "No offense. I'm going to call it quits."

"No offense taken," Slocum said. He had eight dollars more than when he had started, and guessed the gambler had twice that, having been in the game longer. Since the man wasn't leaving with any of Slocum's money, and there hadn't been any cheating going on—there was no call to cheat since the cowboys played so poorly—Slocum was content to switch to whiskey and then find a place to curl up for the night. In the morning, some of the money he'd won would be put onto some swayback nag's purchase price so he could keep riding.

The gambler cast a quick glance over his shoulder, then evaporated like rain in the desert, choosing to go out the saloon's back door. Slocum looked at the double swinging doors to see what had spooked the man. A short Mexican wearing a huge sombrero and a vaquero's getup swaggered into the saloon. The man was maybe thirty, had a pencil-thin black mustache, and couldn't have stood taller than a short drink of water. Slocum was six foot even, and this vaquero was a foot shorter and ten times as arrogant.

"I am here!" the vaquero cried. "I am here! Serve me your best, for it is barely good enough for me!"

"You got money, I'll give you a shot. You don't have money, then get the hell out," the barkeep said.

Slocum rocked back in his chair to watch the show. The vaquero put his hand on the butt of his six-gun, threatening the barkeep. As provocative as the move was, the barkeep didn't flinch.

"You don't have no bullets for that hogleg," he said. "And I bet you don't have money for a drink neither."

"I, Don Rodrigo de la Madrid y Garza, have money!" He fumbled in a vest pocket and produced a nickel. *"Cerveza, por favor!"*

"Here you go," the barkeep said, making sure he had his money before sliding the beer mug across to the vaquero.

Slocum sipped the rest of his whiskey, then got to his feet. It was time to find a place to sleep. If he could convince the livery stable owner to let him use a stall with some fresh straw, he might wrangle a deal for a horse in the morning. He tossed back the rest of his whiskey and rocked forward so all four chair legs sat firmly on the floor. A hulking cowboy slammed the swinging doors open and clanked in just then, his spurs jangling. He was already drunk, and the doors were hardly wide enough for him to stumble through. He looked around, but stopped when he saw the vaquero nursing his beer at the bar.

Slocum remained seated as he watched. He had seen men like this before, and they meant nothing but trouble for most folks around them. The way the barkeep shrank back told Slocum the newcomer was mean enough for two.

"Now lookee here. What we got? A greaser thinkin' he's as good as a white man. You a Meskin? From that rig, I say you are."

"I am," the vaquero said.

"I heard tell you Meskins like to dance. Show me."

"I can dance the fandango with the best." The vaquero turned to face the cowboy. Looking straight ahead, he stared into the man's chest. The vaquero's eyes worked up.

"Dance for me."

"I do not dance for you or with you, should you be of that kind."

Slocum moved to slip the leather thong off the hammer of his Colt Navy. This wasn't his fight, but he wasn't going to sit and get filled with lead if the two got into a shooting match.

"You callin' me a fancy boy?"

"You know what you are," the vaquero said.

"You two take it on outside. I don't want—" The barkeep clamped his mouth shut when the cowboy growled deep in his throat like a hungry wolf.

"Me and this greaser, we got an insult to settle."

"I do not insult such as you," the vaquero said. "It is beneath me."

With a roar, the burly cowboy grabbed the vaquero and lifted him off the floor. He began shaking him like a terrier with a rat in its teeth, then threw him across the saloon with contemptuous ease.

"You go for that gun of yours. Don't matter to me if you do, since I'm gonna cut you down."

"I have no bullets," the vaquero said, sitting on the floor.

"Then I guess I gotta share. One bullet at a time. Where you want the first one? In your balls? Naw, that wouldn't hurt you none. Might be I ought to give you the first bullet in the gut. Or your kneecap?"

The cowboy started to draw, but found he couldn't pull his six-gun from its holster. Slocum's iron grip on his wrist prevented it.

"You'd shoot a man who just said he didn't have any bullets?"

"Who the hell are you?" With a bull-throated, drunken roar, the cowboy heaved and broke Slocum's grip. "You takin' the part of a greaser?"

Slocum stepped in and swung. His fist traveled only a foot, but it ended up buried wrist deep in the man's gut. The man gasped, bent forward, and then began gagging. Slocum grabbed him by the collar, steered him toward the door, and gave him a shove out into the street.

"You have saved me from having to do him great harm, Señor. For this, I give you thanks and offer you the position of foreman on my hacienda."

"Not interested," Slocum said. He tried to keep from laughing at the vaquero. The man's threadbare clothing told more than words ever could about his supposed wealth. "I don't need a job."

"If you do, I, Don Rodrigo de la Madrid y Garza, will see that you are installed as a prince!" The Mexican pulled himself up to his full height, smoothed his permanently wrinkled, filthy shirt, and strode from the saloon, head held high. If attitude meant anything, he was the richest man in all Mexico.

Slocum did laugh then.

"You didn't do nobody any favors, mister," the barkeep said when he got the nerve to come over. "That was El Loco. Leastways, that's what we call him around Eagle Pass."

"He's a mite touched in the head?"

"More than a mite," the barkeep said. "But he's a harmless cayuse. Not the other one."

"The drunk?"

"You better think on gettin' out of town as fast as you can. He's a mean one liquored up or sober. His boss is even meaner 'n a stepped-on rattlesnake. As soon shoot you in the back as spit on you."

Slocum shrugged it off. He heard such tales everywhere he went.

"In the morning, when I get another horse, I'll be leaving, and not a second before," he said. The expression on the barkeep's face told him how foolish this was, but Slocum was bone-tired from tramping through the desert, and the run-in with the drunk had not done much to put him in a good mood. The only moment that hadn't been life-or-death serious had come from El Loco, as he had been monickered.

Slocum went outside into the cold night air. The sudden gust of frigid wind off the desert wiped away any of the fog of beer and booze that remained. With the alcoholic haze went the anesthetic value, leaving behind aches, pains, and the reminder of how footsore he was after his hike.

He bent to pick up his saddle, then decided against it. The reflection in the saloon window showed a tall man out in the street, feet squared and his hand lingering over his six-shooter. Slocum straightened and turned, glad that he had not bothered putting the leather keeper back on the hammer of his own six-gun.

"You the one what whupped up on Luther? Get your sorry ass out here where I can see you."

"Who's Luther? The drunk I threw out of the saloon?"

"I'm Duke Denham." The way the huge man spoke said that he was a gunman with some reputation in town. Having a reputation in Eagle Pass didn't impress Slocum at all.

He stepped out into the dirt and walked up to where he could look Denham in the eye. The man stood a couple inches taller, had a pink scar running along his right cheek, and nervously curled and uncurled his fingers over the butt of his six-shooter.

"You get that in a knife fight?" Slocum asked.

"What? What do you mean?"

"The scar on your cheek," Slocum said, stepping closer. The instant Denham started to touch the scar with his fingers, Slocum moved as fast as lightning. He had poked Luther in the belly, but Luther had been drunk and obviously sported a beer gut. Denham looked to be in better shape, so Slocum aimed his fist at the man's exposed Adam's apple.

He connected and felt cartilage break. Denham gagged and grabbed for his damaged throat. Slocum gauged his distance and swung again, this time connecting with the point of the man's jaw. The shock went all the way up to Slocum's shoulder, but the other man gave a soft sigh and collapsed into a heap in the middle of the street.

"Son of a bitch," Slocum said, shaking his hand. He rubbed his knuckles to ease the pain. He hadn't broken any bones, and for that he was thankful. When he turned, he faced a large crowd of men all silently staring at him.

He got ready to draw.

2

Slocum took a deep breath and exhaled slowly to calm himself. Against a couple dozen men, many weighed down on their hips with hardware, he had to pick and choose his shots carefully. If he figured out who the leader was, that was where his first round would be aimed. Then Slocum would have to simply keep firing until the crowd either cut and ran or killed him.

His eyes widened and he stood a little straighter when a couple of the men began clapping. The sentiment spread quickly. He was almost deafened by both the applause and the loud cheering that followed.

"Good going, mister!" "You shoulda kilt the bastard!" "You're a hero come to Eagle Pass!"

Slocum had no idea what to say, so he simply stared at the men. As if this were a signal, they rushed forward. He restrained his hand from whipping out his six-shooter, but all the men wanted to do was clap him on the back and shake his hand.

"You're one in a million, mister. Ain't nobody ever laid Duke Denham out like that," said a grizzled old man so humped up with arthritis he could barely move. "Come on into the saloon and let me buy you a drink. Whiskey!"

A cheer went up. Slocum stepped over Denham, who was making tiny mewling sounds now as he writhed about on the ground clutching his damaged throat.

"Think somebody should fetch the marshal and have him put into jail?" Slocum asked.

"He didn't do nuthin' to break the law," said the old man shuffling ahead of Slocum. As he turned to hold the door open, he exposed his chest. Slocum saw the glint of pale coal oil light from within reflect off a battered tin badge.

"You're the law in these parts?" Slocum stared. The old man couldn't handle a newborn kitten, much less an owl-hoot like Denham.

"That I am, and after you let me buy you a drink, might be you'd consent to bein' deputized. I surely can use some help."

Slocum looked at the other men crowding into the saloon. Not a one of them looked at him now. The mere notion of being made a deputy erased all trace of backbone in them.

"Don't suppose anybody else ever stood up to him," Slocum said. He took his shot of whiskey. It burned all the way down his gullet and puddled in his belly. He had the offer of a dozen more drinks, but he was careful how fast he drank now. If Denham was as ornery as the towns-people made him out to be, he was likely to want a rematch, this time with six-shooters blazing. Slocum needed a steady hand and a sharp eye the rest of the time he was in Eagle Pass.

Which would be until morning and he found a horse to ride out on.

"You're the first," said the marshal. "He's about the nasti-est outlaw in these parts. I complain all the time to the boys in blue up at Fort Davis, but they don't want to do nuthin' but hunt fer Injuns."

Slocum knew which was more important. Finding the Apaches and getting them back onto their reservation was a bigger chore than cleaning up the mess a petty outlaw like Duke Denham might leave. The citizens of Eagle Pass didn't see it that way, but they weren't under attack by Victorio's band of renegades either.

"I don't care much for pinning on a badge, Marshal," he said honestly. "Eagle Pass happened to be in my path. That's all."

"How come you carried your saddle into town?" asked another man. He was old, too, but stood upright and had a glint in his eye that told Slocum never to play poker with him. He was as sharp in the brain as he was a dresser, and he was something of a fashion plate, which made him stand out in the crowd.

"Horse died under me," Slocum said. He didn't want to get into an involved storytelling session. He guessed most of the men in this room had tales to tell of being bullied by Denham and Luther and the rest of that gang. Hearing the stories would obligate him, in their minds, to taking the job offered by their town marshal.

"Do tell. My men spotted some Apaches out on the road from San Antone yesterday. Wouldn't have anything to do with them, now would it?" When Slocum didn't answer, the man went on. "One of the canteens you've got with your gear's government issue. Could it be you got some water from a patrol out of Fort Davis?"

"You have a sharp eye, sir," Slocum said.

"I have need of a sharpshooter. You have the look about you." The older man's eyes drifted to Slocum's six-gun, and then came back to lock with his emerald green eyes. "Yes, I certainly do have need of a man capable of handling himself."

"Yup, that there's Jonah Rasumussen," the marshal said proudly, as if this explained everything. When he saw that the name didn't spark any recognition, he went on. "Mr. Rasumussen's the Butterfield Stage agent here in town. If it weren't for the stagecoach, why, Eagle Pass might just dry up and blow away."

"Dry up," Slocum said. He took another shot of whiskey and downed it. He had the feeling he was going to need more before this evening was over.

"Now, you don't have a horse, you borrowed a canteen from the cavalry, and the Butterfield Stagecoach Company's got a standing contract for any and all horses in Eagle Pass," Rasumussen said. He waited for this to sink in.

"No amount of money's going to buy me a horse, is that it?"

"Well, sir, if anybody sold you a horse, that'd be in violation of the contract Butterfield has signed with the town of Eagle Pass. I'd have to report such a breach of contract."

"It'd never stand up in court," Slocum said.

"You're right, but the company might think again on where they want a depot. Some town," Rasumussen said, his voice booming now, "where they honored their contracts."

"Does being a deputy mean I'd get a horse?" he asked the marshal.

"Well, sir, that ain't never come up before. Never had a deputy before. I reckon the answer'd be no. The town don't have spare horses. Like Mr. Rasumussen said, all the nags are spoken for."

"It's not likely the Butterfield Stagecoach Company would part with a horse either, is it?" Slocum and Rasumussen looked at each other.

"No reason to have a horse if you're riding the stage as a shotgun guard," Rasumussen said. "Been too long since we had a decent guard riding alongside old Smitty."

"Could a man work for Butterfield long enough to earn a horse as pay?"

"A month," Rasumussen said, stroking his neatly trimmed, gray-shot beard. "Yep, that'd be about right. A month of riding shotgun messenger would earn a fellow room, board, two dollars a week—and a horse."

"When's the next stage?" Slocum asked. He didn't like being boxed in like this, but he hadn't been going anywhere in particular either. Another month, with a job, to earn a horse seemed reasonable.

"Tomorrow morning, dawn. Welcome to working for the Butterfield Stage Company." Rasumussen thrust out his hand. Slocum shook it.

The six-horse team neighed and tried to buck. The young man who had hitched them up walked back and forth, and finally grabbed the harness between the two lead horses and held them steady, speaking quietly to them until the spirited team was settled down and ready to pull. Only then did the man come around to where Slocum prepared to climb into the driver's box with his rifle.

"Where you goin', mister?"

"Up."

"No, you ain't. This here's my stage."

"You must be Smitty," Slocum said. The man was hardly into his twenties. From the way Rasumussen had spoken, he thought the driver was going to be older than the marshal.

"That's who I am. That don't answer who you might be."

"Smitty, I see you've met your new guard," Jonah Rasumussen said, coming from the depot. "He'll be riding with you for a month or so."

"Don't need nobody else," the driver said.

From the sullen way Smitty spoke, Slocum guessed why he didn't want any company in the driver's box. He was drawing double pay for both driving and being shotgun messenger.

"I won't get in your way," Slocum said. "From what Rasumussen is paying me, he can probably see fit to give you something extra to put up with me." He saw that he had hit the nail on the head from Rasumussen's frown and the way Smitty brightened.

"How about that, Mr. Rasumussen?"

"Very well. Now stop yammering and get the strongbox

loaded. The passengers are anxious to get on the road to El Paso."

"Ain't nobody's ever anxious to get to El Paso," Smitty said. Slocum had to laugh at that. He had been through the dirty border town often enough to know this was probably right. Franklin, where he had been heading when the Apaches shot his horse, was little better.

"I'll get the strongbox loaded," Slocum said. "Up in the driver's box or back in the boot?"

"Back," said Smitty. "You don't want to rupture yourself hoistin' that box too far. Never know what we got in it. Sometimes I think Rasumussen sends it with lead bricks just to bedevil me." Smitty grinned crookedly. "Now he's got somebody else to bedevil. Get on with it, Slocum, whilst I load the passengers. Sometimes it's like herdin' frightened cattle, other times sheep."

Slocum went into the Butterfield office and saw the heavy iron box on the desk. It had two large straps riveted around it, and a huge padlock held the hasp in a firm metallic grip.

"Anything inside worth dying for?" Slocum asked.

"There always is. No other private company moves valuables up and down this side of Texas the way we do," Rasumussen said.

Slocum grabbed the box and lifted. He almost dropped it. He had expected it to have some heft, but not this much. He began to appreciate what Smitty said about getting a rupture carrying the box out to the stagecoach. Getting a better grip, Slocum heaved and staggered under the weight. Wrestling it onto the ledge at the back of the stage with the passengers' luggage proved a chore, but Slocum finally secured it with chains anchored to the body of the stagecoach.

"You ready, Slocum? Then get on up here. We're already late, and this driver don't cotton to ever bein' even a minute late." Smitty uncurled a blacksnake whip and gave it a twitch with his wrist that curled it about in nervous circles.

Slocum glanced into the passenger compartment and saw three men, all looking as if they had already ridden a hundred miles that morning. He didn't bother telling them what they already knew. When the sun climbed higher in the sky, that stage compartment would turn into a hotbox. If they lowered the leather curtains, they would cook. If they didn't, the dust would choke them to death.

He caught at the side of the coach and pulled himself up. He settled his rifle, and was thrown backward as Smitty snapped the whip and got the team pulling in unison. A few more expert snaps was all it took to keep the horses at a steady gait. Smitty put the whip back into a holder at his left knee and took the reins in both hands.

Slocum appreciated Smitty's expertise and reminded himself that a man's ability had nothing to do with his age. The Eagle Pass marshal was older than dirt and ineffectual, where Smitty was hardly dry behind the ears and an experienced stagecoach driver.

Slocum settled back, pulled up his bandanna to cover his mouth and nose against the invasive dust, and kept an eye peeled for any movement out across the arid terrain.

He spotted the ambush an hour down the road.

"Up ahead," Slocum warned.

"Don't see it," Smitty said, casting a sidelong glance at Slocum as if accusing him of falling victim to a mirage.

Slocum hefted his rifle and levered a round into the chamber. The stagecoach bucked and lurched as Smitty kept the horses pulling as hard as they could in the heat, making Slocum's aim shaky. He judged the up-and-down motion, then squeezed off a round. The Winchester bucked and a slow smile came to his lips.

"Got one."

"You got shit out there. That's . . . oh, my God!" Smitty finally spotted the masked road agents waiting in an arroyo. The road dipped through the dry channel and then came out on the other side. He had to slow the horses to navigate the narrow, treacherous road. If he stopped in the bottom of the arroyo, chances were good the stage would get stuck in the shifting sand.

Slocum got off another shot that did nothing but scare the outlaws' horses. That was almost as good as killing them. The masked men fought to keep their mounts from bolting. Slocum got off three more shots, and then the stage hit the arroyo and almost tossed him from the driver's box.

Smitty used his blacksnake whip to force the horses through the soft footing. Then another jolt rattled Slocum's teeth, and he knew they were up the far side of the arroyo and once more on sunbaked road. He flopped onto the top of the stage and fired a few more times, but the outlaws had lost all taste for robbery.

"You got eyes like a hawk," Smitty said. "I didn't spot 'em till almost too late."

"That's why I'm along," Slocum said, settling back onto the hardwood bench seat. He carefully pulled cartridges from his coat pocket and reloaded. "I recognized one of them."

"What? How could you? They was wearin' masks."

"Duke Denham wore a shirt back in town exactly like the one on the gang's leader. Not enough proof to hold up in court maybe, but enough to make me wary around him." Slocum lowered the hammer on his rifle and added, "More wary than before, that is. The bartender at the Hijinx said Luther was bad medicine and that Denham was worse."

"Heard how you coldcocked that son of a bitch. Thought it was a bit of tall tale tellin', but I see Rasumussen wasn't exaggeratin' none."

"There many robberies on this road?"

"There's a reason why I haven't had a guard these past weeks," Smitty said, the muscles standing out in bold relief on his forearms and shoulders as he wrestled with the six-horse team. "We was robbed and the outlaws shot down my guard without so much as a fare-thee-well. He didn't do nuthin'. He dropped his gun, grabbed some sky, and they just shot him. I have to tell you, I was a'feared for my life."

"The marshal's got to know Duke Denham is out robbing stages. Why doesn't he do anything about it?"

"Marshal Atkinson's an old man. All he wants to do is set around his office, suck his gums, and read penny dreadfuls."

"Leastways, he can read. That's more than you can say for most marshals."

Smitty laughed at this.

"You got a weird sense of humor, Slocum. I like that. But yeah, Atkinson'd rather have his nose stuck in a book than be out enforcin' what's in them law books of his. On average, I'd say three stages a month get robbed on this here road. With the Apaches rovin' about, I'm surprised more ain't robbed."

"There's nothing on a stagecoach an Indian would want 'less it was water. They don't put much store in gold," Slocum said.

"Damned savages," Smitty said. "Scalpin' folks and not even wantin' to steal their gold after they do." He shook his head and went back to tugging on the reins to control the team.

"Slow down," Slocum said after they had gone another half dozen miles.

"Need to make up time. There's a way station not a mile off. The passengers need a break, and I have to get a new team if we're gonna make it to Fort Davis 'fore sundown."

"Slow down," Slocum repeated. He braced himself against the swaying motion as he pulled down the brim of his hat to shade his eyes. He got a better look at the man smack in the middle of the road ahead, a six-shooter drawn and waving about in the air. "We've got ourselves another road agent."

"Damnation, this is not my day. I get a bonus if I get the passengers to their destination on time. Slowing down for even a minute's gonna cost me a dollar a head."

"This won't take too long."

"What do you mean?"

"Stop the stage. I'll go talk to the road agent."

Smitty looked at Slocum as if the heat had finally boiled away what few brains he had, but pulling back powerfully on the reins slowed and finally halted the horses.

"Back in a minute."

"You're gonna dicker with him? An outlaw?"

"Something like that," Slocum said. He didn't bother taking his rifle as he walked ahead of the stagecoach.

"You will stand and deliver!" the road agent cried. "I will take your gold for my own!"

"Afternoon," Slocum said, taking off his hat and slapping the dust off it. He carefully put it back on and faced the mounted rider. "You been out in the heat too long, Señor de la Madrid?"

"You know me? Even with my mask hiding my face, you know of me? My fame has indeed spread throughout all of Texas!"

"Trying to rob a stage is a good way to get yourself killed."

El Loco pulled down his mask and stared at Slocum, seeing him clearly for the first time.

"I know you! I have offered you the job of foreman on my hacienda. Have you stopped me to accept my generous offer of employment?"

"Got a job," Slocum said.

"You may call me Don Rodrigo."

"My job's to shoot anybody trying to rob the stage. We're in something of a hurry, so I'd be much obliged if we could drive on past. If that's all right with you, Don Rodrigo."

"Why, yes, *sí,* I will permit it."

"That's for the best."

"Remember, Señor, that you have been stopped by the greatest of all *bandidos, el ladrón de todos los ladrones.* I am Don Rodrigo de la Madrid y Garza!"

"You might want to take a break and find yourself a saloon to get the taste of dust out of your mouth," Slocum
suggested.

"You will buy me such a drink? I have left all my *dinero*
back at my vast hacienda."

"When our paths cross again, Don Rodrigo, but only if
you stop trying to rob stagecoaches."

"That is a good idea. I will do that. *Buenas tardes!*" With
that, El Loco rode off eastward. As far as Slocum knew,
nothing but parched desert lay in that direction. He hoped
Don Rodrigo had plenty of water because if he didn't, he
would die a quick death.

Slocum tramped back and pulled himself up into the
driver's box and settled beside Smitty.

The driver's eyes were wide with admiration.

"Never in all my born days have I seen anyone talk a
road agent out of a robbery. You're one hell of a marksman
and you got a silver tongue to boot."

Slocum said nothing, preferring to let Smitty think there
had been some skill involved in convincing a man touched
in the head that he ought to let the stagecoach go on its
way.

As they rattled along, though, Slocum began to worry
about Don Rodrigo and what the desert could do to a man
alone. It didn't even have to drive him mad first. The Mexican was already crazy as a bedbug.

3

"You sure about all that, Slocum?" Marshal Atkinson sucked on his gums as he thought hard on everything Slocum had told him about the two attempted robberies.

Slocum had not wanted to even mention El Loco since he hardly believed the man intended to rob the stage. He had gotten a wild hair up his ass that he was some kind of *bandido* and had taken it into his head to stick up the stage. From all that Slocum could tell after asking around town, nobody had ever seen Don Rodrigo with bullets in his six-gun. The man was harmless.

"As sure as I can be without seeing their faces," Slocum said. "The leader of the road agents wore a shirt that looked about the same as the one Duke Denham wore the night I had my run-in with him."

"Don't much see that color shirt in these parts," Atkinson allowed. Slocum saw how uneasy the lawman was even talking about Denham and his gang. While the road agent was inept, he had to be a major threat to a backwater town like Eagle Pass.

"You can tell the Rangers about him. If Denham is as dangerous as you say, they must want him something fierce."

"Used the telegraph," Atkinson said. "The Ranger headquarters wired back they didn't have no wanted posters on him."

"That's hard to believe, a man who prides himself on being so tough." Slocum wondered how much of a desperado Duke Denham actually was if the Texas Rangers weren't after him.

"You might say, around Eagle Pass he's a big frog in a small pond. He leaves here, well—" Marshal Atkinson shrugged his arthritic shoulders. Slocum got the meaning. Denham might stay in the region because he was a feared outlaw here, but if he roved anywhere else, he would be beneath contempt of real outlaws—and real lawmen.

"He's going to kill somebody," Slocum said.

"I'll go after him. By jiminy, I will!"

"You thinking on a posse? There might be a few men willing to go after Denham."

"Denham? I meant El Loco. We can nab him 'fore he sneaks back across the Rio Grande to safety."

"He's harmless," Slocum said. "I talked him out of robbing the stage. What sort of real robber lets anybody talk him out of getting rich using his six-shooter?"

"I want somebody to toss into the jail. The townspeople need to know I ain't just sittin' 'round doin' nuthin' but suckin' on the public teat."

Slocum listened to the pathetic speech but held his tongue. As far as he could see, this was exactly what the marshal did. He read his cheap books, he prowled about in the evenings cadging drinks from the town's three saloons, and he didn't do a whole lot else. The crowd's applause still rang in Slocum's ears after he had laid Duke Denham low. They had finally seen an outlaw get his comeuppance after the law wouldn't do anything about him.

"I need to check with Rasumussen about the next shipment," Slocum said. He wanted to let the marshal come to his senses about putting a posse onto El Loco's trail. He thought the lawman would forget about it entirely, given enough time.

"You do that, Slocum, but I'll want you in the posse. You talked him out of a robbery. You might talk him into a cell without a whole lot of gunfightin'."

Slocum closed the jailhouse door behind him. The heat tore at his face and sucked the sweat off his leathery skin to cool him a mite. It was a good four hours until sundown and the coolness that came with it. He settled his six-shooter and started for the Hijinx Saloon to partake of a drink or two. Now that he was earning money, even the pittance Jonah Rasumussen paid him to keep him going until he earned his horse, he felt better about downing whiskey rather than beer.

"You. You're the one!"

Slocum stopped and looked around. A woman in an alley stared at him with wide-set brown eyes. She was in her early twenties, short, with long dark hair and the arrogance born of money. In spite of that attitude, she was dressed as a peon. With hands on her flaring hips, she boldly challenged him with her words.

"I reckon I might be the one. That depends on what one you're looking for."

"You are John Slocum, the one who stopped the stagecoach robbery."

"I'm the guard," he said carefully, not knowing what she wanted from him. "Just got back into town after a week on the road."

"But you stopped the robbery?"

"I winged one of the road agents," he said. The horror on the lovely woman's face caused him to suck in a breath and hold it for a moment. It wasn't the reaction he expected. She couldn't be a stranger to a bit of gunfighting. When anyone looked as fine she did, gunfire usually ensued between suitors.

"You shot Rodrigo?"

"Don Rodrigo?" Slocum laughed. "I talked him out of the robbery, if you want to call it that. The other outlaws, the ones who had tried a little while before him, I shot one of them and drove the rest off."

"Rodrigo is unharmed?"

"As far as I know. When we drove past him, he was hale and hearty, though that might not have lasted long since he was riding out into the desert without enough water."

"But you did not shoot him?"

"Truth is, I tried to steer him in the direction of some town where he could buy a beer, or at least get a glass of water."

"They do not understand Rodrigo here. He must be taken home."

"Across the Rio Grande?"

"He is a Mexican."

"What's he to you?" Slocum studied the woman's face and knew the answer to his question before she spoke.

"I am Consuela de la Madrid y Garza, his sister."

"That brings up another question," he said. This confused her.

"What is this?"

"How can such an ugly gent have such a pretty sister?"

For an instant, Consuela simply stared at him. Then she laughed. It was deep and rich and genuine.

"I have not been mistaken about you," she said. "You argue for my brother, not against him."

"The marshal wants a posse to go after road agents, your brother being the one he's most interested in arresting."

"Because other *bandidos* would shoot back? Poor Rodrigo has to cadge drinks. He has no bullets for his pistol."

She spoke, but Slocum was hardly listening. Some silent communication passed between the two that made words meaningless. He had seldom seen a woman as lovely, but he had found the most beautiful were the most treacherous. He got none of that feeling from Consuela. If anything, he felt drawn to her in ways all too familiar and completely unreasonable since they had met only minutes earlier. She was refined, not some barroom whore to be bought for a quarter.

"I know what you are thinking, John Slocum," she said, stepping closer.

"I doubt you do," he said. He saw how Consuela tipped her head back slightly. Her red lips parted as her eyes closed. He kissed her hard and she kissed back with equal passion. They clung to each other until they lost their balance and crashed against the brick wall of a bakery. The bricks were warm behind Slocum's back, and he heard the sounds of men working inside to bake bread for the morning. The sweet smells of the bread mingled with the wine taste of Consuela's lips and the warm, urgent feel of her body against his.

She pressed closer to him. His hand moved downward until he cupped her firm buttocks and began to squeeze slowly, sensuously. She moaned and moved even closer until her taut breasts flattened against his chest.

"I was wrong," he said. "You did know what I was thinking."

"I am a good girl. I do not do this with a man I have just met."

He silenced her protests with another kiss because he knew this was what she wanted. No talk. Just action. His hands slowly pulled up her flowing, ornately decorated skirt until he felt the firm brown flesh trembling under his fingers. He parted those luscious half-moons and let his finger explore more. He found her wet nether lips and poked between them.

"Oh," she said, shuddering at his gentle intrusion. "That feels so . . . small. I want something larger there."

"This?" He thrust in two fingers, then three.

"This," she said, arching her back so she could work her hands between them. She dropped his gun belt and then unfastened the buttons on his fly. His erection popped out into the warmth of her fingers curled about it. A few quick strokes and Slocum knew he was as hard as he ever could be. Then she proved him wrong. Consuela lifted one leg and hooked it around his waist, pressing her crotch into his. They both gasped as he sank deeply into her molten center.

He dipped down and then straightened his legs, giving a short stroking action to his hidden manhood. She began tensing and relaxing herself around him, making the fit even tighter and more arousing. Slocum had thought he was as hard as he could get. The slow movement coupled with her knowing massage proved him wrong. He ached he was so hard. His balls tightened until he felt like a stick of dynamite ready to explode.

He lifted her entirely off the ground so she could hook her legs half around him, her heels pressed into the backs of his knees. Leaning against the wall for support, he arched his back while Consuela rotated her hips. The dual motion was all it took for him to get off. He felt the fierce tide mounting within him and then he erupted. He kissed her face and lips and neck as she tossed her head about and stifled her cries of passion.

When they both felt their muscles relaxing from their ultimate pleasures, Slocum dipped down and put her onto the ground. Together, they slid to sit on the ground, the bakery behind them. They did not look at each other but out into Eagle Pass's deserted main street.

Finally, Slocum said, "I know you're not the kind. I apologize."

"You should," she said primly. "You have not made another move for me in minutes!"

Slocum looked at her and saw she was only half joking. She still felt the way he had. There was a powerful attraction between the two of them neither could deny. He found himself wanting to go to the hotel, get a room with a bed, and then see how loud the springs would squeak for the rest of the night. But that wasn't going to happen. He doubted any hotel there would allow Mexicans in, and he wouldn't want to gun down a clerk over it.

Or maybe he would. Consuela made him feel that way.

"We should not be seen like this," she said, smoothing her skirt. She looked up at him. "I would see you naked."

A slow smile came to his lips. Slocum nodded and pointed toward the hotel. Consuela shook her head.

"Not there. They do not like Mexicans."

"I can make them," he said.

"No, no, here." She bent and picked up his discarded gun belt and handed it to him. "I will show you a place." Together, they walked away from Eagle Pass, going into the rocky hills not far off where she had pitched a camp. The small fire had died down to fitful coals, but she quickly built the fire again until Slocum was feeling uncomfortable standing near it. Consuela grinned at him.

"If it is so hot, take off your clothes," she said.

"You'll do anything to get me naked. What'll it take to get you out of yours?"

"Ask."

He did.

"I should join the posse," Slocum said. He sipped at the hot coffee Consuela had made for breakfast. The rest of her larder was mighty empty, but Slocum couldn't complain after the night they had spent together.

"You would capture my brother?" She looked at him with her hot eyes. There was no passion for him there now. Only anger smoldered.

"I'm not as likely as Marshal Atkinson to take a potshot at Don Rodrigo."

"Don Rodrigo," she said, laughing ruefully. "Why does he say such things? They can only get him into trouble."

"All the more reason to lock him up rather than string him up," Slocum said. "A posse in these parts doesn't get paid unless they find a criminal. The marshal's not likely to tangle with Duke Denham, so that leaves only one road agent."

"Rodrigo is no thief. He pretends. Always, all he does is

pretend. Make-believe. He thinks he is a gunfighter. Then he says he is a robber. Whatever comes into his mind, that is what he wants to be." She threw out her coffee and stared into the fire.

"I won't let anything happen to him. When I bring him back, you'll be here?"

"Do you want me to be?"

"I'd like that," Slocum said. "You should also be here to take charge of him, being family and all."

"I will see him back to the family across the Rio Grande," Consuela said. "You will do this for me?"

"For Don Rodrigo," he said. Slocum had taken a fancy to the loco El Loco.

"Yes, for Don Rodrigo," she said in resignation. Then she became more animated and kissed him.

Slocum considered all the things he could do, then reluctantly got to his feet. He had to return to town or the posse would ride without him.

He trooped down the main street to the marshal's office. Atkinson already had rounded up three cowboys, who stood laughing and joking outside the office. Inside were two more, being deputized.

"Slocum, you decided to tag along?" Atkinson asked, coming out.

"I'm a decent enough tracker," Slocum said. "I feel more comfortable leading rather than following."

"Reckon that might be true. You just be sure you're on El Loco's trail. There's plenty of others out there we don't want to tangle with," the lawman said. He rubbed at his watery eyes and looked a hundred years old.

"Like Duke Denham?"

"The Apaches. Let the cavalry run them down. That's not our fight. El Loco is. He tried to rob the stage."

"Why not worry about crimes that are committed rather than only attempted?" Slocum asked.

Marshal Atkinson took Slocum by the arm and led him

out of earshot of the five cowboys, all trying to impress one another with their shiny deputy's badges.

"It's like this, Slocum. It ain't no secret that Eagle Pass could have a better marshal 'n me. I can't stand up to bullies like Denham. The notion of even seeing a Warm Springs Apache makes me fill both boots with my own piss. But they pay me and there's gotta be some criminal brought to justice."

"Why El Loco?" Slocum knew the answer even as the question escaped his lips. Don Rodrigo was an easy target. Without bullets, he wasn't likely to harm anybody and Atkinson would have someone behind bars who had almost committed a crime. "Never mind," Slocum said. "Let's get on the trail before it's too hot."

"Ain't never gonna be like that," Atkinson said. "Always too somethin'. Too hot, too cold, too windy, too dusty. That's West Texas in a nutshell." He put his fingers in his mouth and let out a surprisingly loud whistle that got the attention of his five deputies. "Let's ride, boys. We got a desperado to find."

Slocum stood and waited for Atkinson to ask why he wasn't mounted and ready to go.

"My horse was shot out from under me before I got to Eagle Pass," he said. "Rasumussen claims all the spare horses in town belong by contract to the Butterfield Company. If you want me in the posse, you have to give me a horse."

"I got a spare," said one cowboy. "You can't have her, but you can ride her."

This had to do. Slocum had hoped to cadge a horse from the marshal and maybe keep on riding once they got away from town. However, the night he had spent with Consuela made simply stealing the horse a little more difficult, because he felt he owed her. Returning her crazy brother where she could watch him was the least of it.

"Where do we head, Slocum?"

Slocum got on the road going up to Fort Davis and

passed the spot where Duke Denham and his gang had tried to rob the stagecoach. He stopped the posse there, amid much grumbling because the sun beat down almost directly on the tops of their heads, and prowled about until he found evidence that Denham had hightailed it toward the Rio Grande. This section of the desert was flat and sandy, but a few miles away rocky foothills built into low mountains mighty fast. Slocum guessed that Denham had a hideout in the winding canyons where he could post lookouts to warn of any approaching posse. Slocum almost led the marshal in that direction, then discarded the notion as too dangerous. At the first whine of lead through the air, Atkinson and the cowboys would hightail it.

"What you findin', Slocum?" Atkinson sounded uneasy.

"Nothing. You see anything?"

"Nary a thing."

"Marshal, we're gonna head on back to town," one cowboy said. "There ain't nuthin' to find out here."

"Git on back," Atkinson said glumly. "Me and Slocum'll find El Loco if you too scared."

"Ain't scared, just thirsty," the man said. The other newly deputized lawmen all agreed.

"Go on, get out of my sight, but you don't get paid nuthin'!" Marshal Atkinson said. He growled deep in his throat like a dog facing down a coyote. The deputies turned their horses back toward Eagle Pass and were out of sight within a few minutes.

"So, Slocum, you got any notion where he is or are we just wastin' time like they thought?"

Slocum was willing to lead the marshal around in circles, but his heart sank when he spotted El Loco. The Mexican vaquero crested a rise not a quarter mile away. The sunlight glinted off the battered conchas on the man's pants and sombrero. Even a man as blind as Marshal Atkinson would have been hard-pressed to miss him, especially since Don Rodrigo took off his sombrero and waved it around.

Atkinson cast a quick look at Slocum, then put his heels to his horse's flanks. Slocum had no choice but to ride along, if only to keep either Rodrigo or the marshal from getting hurt accidentally. He doubted either could hit the side of a barn if they were locked inside, but El Loco hadn't had any bullets. With the marshal spraying lead all around, he was more likely to hit his quarry.

"He's making for Mexico," Atkinson said. "We kin grab him 'fore he gets over the river."

"How far is the Rio Grande?"

"Ten miles, more or less," the marshal said.

"His horse is limping. Got a bad leg. He won't be able to go another mile before the horse pulls up entirely lame."

Atkinson had his head down and rode as if he meant it. They overtook El Loco within minutes and capturing him was all too easy.

"Drop that hogleg of yours," the marshal barked. "I swear, I'll shoot you, you mangy varmint!"

"I? I am this 'mangy varmint' of which you speak? You insult me!"

"Don't," Slocum said, riding between El Loco and the marshal. "Leave your six-shooter in its holster or I'll have to take it away from you."

"He can't be a prisoner and keep his iron," Atkinson protested.

"I'll handle this, Marshal." And Slocum did. It took some sweet-talking, but Slocum convinced El Loco to ride back to Eagle Pass with them—and he did it without ever once mentioning that Consuela was waiting for El Loco.

Slocum thought El Loco was luckier than he had any right to be, having a woman like that wanting to look after him.

4

"Yes, sir, Slocum, I been tellin' ever'one in Eagle Pass how much safer they are. They appreciated it, too, knowin' a dangerous desperado like El Loco is all locked up in the calaboose."

Slocum started to tell Marshal Atkinson what he thought about public safety and having El Loco in a cell, but held his tongue. In a way, things were safer with Don Rodrigo in jail. El Loco wasn't likely to get himself shot trying one of his dumb stunts. Another guard would have taken an easy shot and killed him when he tried to stop the stage. Consuela had said her brother had taken a fancy to proclaiming himself a gunfighter, only he had no bullets in his six-shooter when Atkinson finally captured him. Slocum had made sure and checked.

Slocum snorted at that thought. The marshal had hardly captured anyone. Rodrigo had been ready to come back to town and had thought the marshal was leading a parade. The flights of fancy Don Rodrigo took were wild and varied, and one day would get him killed unless Consuela got him back to his family in Mexico.

"His sister will take him home," Slocum said. "I'll go tell her you have Rodrigo locked up."

"Who? That El Loco's name? Never heard it before," the lawman said, scratching his stubbled chin. He hobbled to his desk and collapsed in the chair. As frail as Atkinson was, the ancient chair still protested even his slight weight. Like everything else in the jailhouse, it was on its last legs. Slocum had checked the jail cell earlier, and wondered who the solitary cell was intended to hold. Bricks in the outer wall were loose, the mortar falling out. With any kind of determined work, a prisoner could get out that way within an hour. In spite of this, Slocum doubted any prisoner would even try since that would require a bit of sweat and work. The rusted lock on the cell door could be opened with a single swift kick.

Atkinson might hold drunks who were too soused to stand, but any serious criminal would be out of the jail before the marshal hung up the key after locking him up.

For Don Rodrigo de la Madrid y Garza, though, the cell would hold him until Consuela could bail him out.

"His sister will take custody of him."

"Custody? What're you goin' on about, Slocum? He ain't goin' nowhere till the circuit judge gets here in a week or two. Then he's gonna be sent down to the prison over yonder in Huntsville. I can see the headlines now. Marshal sends robber to prison!"

"He hasn't robbed any stage. He hasn't done anything but be loco."

"That's fer the jury to decide. Yes, sir, we're gonna have a trial here, you wait and see. You want to be on the jury, Slocum? I got to get to pickin' jurors. Need to scare up the mayor and see what he'll pay. Old man Gross—he owns the Hijinx—will give ever' juror a drink or two. This is gonna be fun, Slocum, the most fun in a month of Sundays."

Disgusted, Slocum left to go tell Consuela that her brother was sound asleep in the cell.

* * *

"Why're you so down in the mouth, Slocum?" Smitty wrestled the last pair of horses into place and fastened the reins. "From all I hear, you're something of a hero."

"What do you mean?" He had told Consuela about her brother, and then had made the mistake of adding that the marshal intended to try Rodrigo for robbery. She had stalked off, as mad at him as she was at Marshal Atkinson. He tried to explain that he had made certain the lawman wouldn't shoot Rodrigo while capturing him, but Consuela wouldn't listen.

"The marshal's tellin' anybody who'll listen how you stood up to El Loco and even marched right on up to him, no matter he had his six-shooter drawn and pointed at you," Smitty added.

"He didn't have any bullets. I knew that, and so did the marshal."

"You couldn't know that," Smitty said. "All it takes is findin' one cartridge to make El Loco a killer." He settled the harness and then patted his lead horse to settle the nervous animal. "Time to roll. Ought to be safer on the road this time, what with El Loco behind bars."

"Yeah, safer," Slocum said. He had underestimated the marshal. The old man might not be able to hold up a six-gun without his arthritic hand shaking, but there was nothing wrong with his tongue or his brain. Atkinson had made Slocum out to be a hero so anything he said later in Don Rodrigo's defense would only seem like he was being modest.

"We got a pair of passengers today," Smitty said. "Look to be a couple peddlers. Need any snake oil?"

"I'm swimming in it," Slocum said. Smitty looked at him curiously, but said nothing more. Slocum went into the depot, and was surprised to see Rasumussen with another man holding a shotgun in the crook of his left arm.

"That's all right, Slocum. He's a guard from San Antone. He brought the strongbox overland in a wagon. From here we get to make sure it arrives in Fort Davis."

A special heavy-duty lock banged against a reinforced hasp when the shotgun-holding guard pushed it in Slocum's direction along the desktop. From the way the box slid, it was heavier than usual, which made it very heavy indeed. Slocum was prepared for the immense weight, and still staggered as he hefted it.

"What do you have in here? A bar of gold?" His comment was innocent enough. Both Rasumussen and the guard jumped as if they had been poked with needles.

"What makes you say that?" The guard swung his shotgun around, but Rasumussen put his hand on the barrel and pushed it so it pointed at the floor rather than at Slocum's head.

"He didn't mean anything by it other than the box is very heavy," the station agent said. "Isn't that right, Slocum?"

Slocum nodded, swung around, and half staggered from the depot to load the strongbox into the stagecoach boot. The back of the stage sagged on the leather straps used as springs. Slocum dusted off his hands and backed away, staring at the box. The only thing that could weigh this much was gold—and a lot of it. He turned and saw Jonah Rasumussen watching him. The stationmaster came over, took Slocum by the arm, and steered him off where they could talk without being overheard.

"You guessed right about the contents, Slocum. That's gold destined for Fort Davis. Not a payroll. The army ships that themselves and it's usually nothing more than scrip. I don't know what this is, but it's something special and it's going to be used to fight the Apaches."

"Bribes?"

Rasumussen shook his head and looked glum.

"I'm not happy having to transport it, but you be on guard every inch of the way. Denham and his gang seem to know when there's something worth stealing on the stage."

Slocum looked around town. Anybody could be a spy for the outlaw. Seeing a particularly heavy strongbox added to the cargo would be like watching ants swarm over a dollop of honey.

"You want more ammo? A scattergun to go along with your rifle?"

"These will do," Slocum said, picking up his Winchester and resting his hand on the butt of his Colt Navy.

"I'll expect you to deliver, and I expect you and Smitty to return without too many extra holes in your worthless hides."

Slocum climbed into the driver's box and settled down alongside Smitty, who was already snapping the reins and itching to be on the road. The sooner they left, the better the chance they had of outrunning the report by Denham's spy. At least, that was the lie Slocum told himself. Duke Denham might not be the brightest son of a bitch around, but he would have worked out a system of rapid communication. A man on a hill outside Eagle Pass with a mirror might be all it took to alert the road agents to a plum waiting to be picked.

Slocum occasionally stood in the pitching driver's box to get a better view of the road ahead and their back trail. He knew that Denham wasn't likely to let them get much past the spot where he had attacked on the last run. The outlaw had worked out a scheme and had been thwarted before. He wasn't the kind to discard a perfectly good plan. The stagecoach had to slow in the deep sand, making it more vulnerable there than at any other spot along the route.

"The arroyo's up ahead," Slocum warned. Smitty never slowed as he raced toward the spot where the road ran through the sandy-bottomed gully. They had to build up enough speed to get through or be mired down.

"You thinkin' what I am, Slocum?"

"That's where we'll be robbed," Slocum said. He brought his rifle up and fired into creosote bushes alongside the road. He had not seen anything, but the wild shot flushed more than a jackrabbit. Two masked men came running out, six-shooters blazing. Slocum kept firing until the road agents veered away and disappeared into the brush. Then the stage hit the arroyo and almost threw Slocum out.

"Hang on, damn you," Smitty cried. "We got more of them varmints ahead."

This time, Slocum was positive he identified Duke Denham. The man was slow pulling up his mask and wore the same shirt he had in town. Slocum concentrated his fire on the outlaw leader and drove him back from the road. As the stagecoach passed the spot where Denham had waited, bullets ripped at the coach from both sides of the road. Slocum lost his hat to a bullet tearing through the brim, and then they were rattling on along the hard road, making good time for Fort Davis.

Not content to let things take their course, Slocum reloaded and then flopped belly down on the roof of the stage and fired at anything looking like a human outline in the dust cloud now obscuring the road.

He finally dropped back alongside the driver and said, "Think we'll run into any more robbers between here and the fort?"

"I hope not. Rasumussen promised me double bonus for getting there on time."

Slocum scowled. Rasumussen had never offered him anything extra for fighting off the road agents so the stage could arrive on time. Then he closed his eyes and tried to roll with the stage as it bounced off rocks and dipped through large potholes. He was getting paid and only a couple more weeks remained before he could earn a horse and be on his way. There wasn't much else he could want.

Somehow, though, he knew there was something more. Consuela. The rest of the trip was spent thinking on her.

"You're sure in a hurry to get back to town, Slocum." Smitty stood up, put his boot against the front of the driver's box, and used this as leverage to slow the team. He expertly brought them to a halt directly in front of the Butterfield depot. They had delivered the strongbox to the paymaster at Fort Davis, dropped off their passengers, and taken on five more. All five were annoying, shouting at Smitty to drive more carefully and at Slocum to keep a sharper lookout for road agents.

"Got a feeling something's happening here," Slocum said.

"You mean you've got a yen for some floozy," Smitty said. "I know the signs. You got that dreamy look and—" The driver stopped when Slocum turned to him and fixed him with a cold stare. "Sorry, Slocum, didn't mean nuthin' by it."

Slocum jumped to the ground, got the two mail sacks they had brought from the cavalry post, and dropped them off with the agent inside the Butterfield office. He looked around for Jonah Rasumussen, but the stationmaster was nowhere to be seen. That hardly mattered to Slocum since he had nothing he wanted to say.

He set off to find Consuela and see if she had gotten her brother out of the town jail in the four days that Slocum had been gone. From the way Marshal Atkinson had spoken about keeping El Loco locked up, Slocum doubted the woman had had much luck. There certainly would never be bail announced. The marshal was nobody's fool and had to know Don Rodrigo would escape across the Rio Grande to be free of gringo justice.

The small camp where the woman had pitched her tent and where she and Slocum had spent the night so pleasurably almost a week earlier was abandoned. He circled the area and found where she had led a horse away. He followed the trail away from town for more than an hour to find Consuela sitting at a fire in a dry arroyo bed, shoulders slumped and completely unaware of anything that went on around her. He got within a few feet before she jerked around, startled.

He stared into her wide brown eyes and saw nothing but anguish.

"The marshal didn't let Rodrigo out on bail," he guessed.

"It is worse than that. Th-they came to my camp. Where we—" She gulped hard and swallowed. Tears trickled down her cheeks. Slocum sank down to sit beside her on a large, smooth rock. He gently wiped away her tears.

"Who came to your camp? Atkinson? Those worthless deputies he took with us when he formed a posse?"

"No, no, not the marshal. Him. He came to my camp and threatened me. He would have raped me if I had not pulled a knife on him. I cut him and got away. When he left, I packed and moved my camp here."

"You weren't hard to track," Slocum said. "Who tried to rape you?"

"Him. Denham!"

Slocum sat a little straighter.

"When?"

"Three days ago. He was furious about something, but when he saw me he became more determined. I tried to lose him in town, but he followed."

Slocum considered the time. He had just prevented Duke Denham and his gang from robbing the stage again. Denham had to have ridden directly into town, intent on taking out his anger on whomever he found. Consuela was a lovely woman, but the way she described him made Slocum wary about jumping to conclusions.

"He saw *you*?"

"Yes, he wanted to ask many questions. He threatened me if I did not tell him about Rodrigo."

Again, Slocum found himself taken down a strange road and becoming even more lost.

"He threatened to rape you if you didn't tell him about your brother?" The woman nodded. "What did he ask about Rodrigo?"

"Crazy things. Denham talked of robberies and killings and wanted to know if Rodrigo had told me anything. I did not have to pretend ignorance. I know nothing. That is when he tried to rape me and I cut him."

"You should have cut his heart out," Slocum said.

"I wanted only to escape."

"He knew your brother was locked up?"

"I never told him. He might not know, but with the marshal saying he has captured a great robber, how can Denham not know?"

Slocum put his arm around the woman's quaking shoulders and held her close. She fit perfectly into the circle of his arms. He felt his shirt turning damp from her tears, but she did not try to pull away and Slocum was not going to push her from him. As Consuela sobbed quietly, Slocum's mind raced. A man like Denham would think nothing of committing rape, but why ask about Don Rodrigo? He had to know Rodrigo was Consuela's brother, or he would not have pursued her and asked about El Loco's whereabouts.

The attempt at rape had come after Consuela had not told him what he wanted to hear.

"He might be mad at your brother for trying to rob the stage," Slocum said. "The attempts put Rasumussen on edge and he told me to keep an eye peeled. Denham failed in his second robbery. He might blame Rodrigo." The words rang hollow in Slocum's ear even as he spoke. Denham and his men were contemptuous of El Loco. They would never bother finding him unless there was something more than simple drunken harassment involved.

"This is all he wanted to know. Where my brother is. I did not tell him."

"Let's hope he didn't find out. He might not want to stick his nose out in Eagle Pass after two failed robberies." Slocum came to a quick decision, and spent the next ten minutes convincing Consuela he meant what he said.

"I will meet you there," she said after he had finished detailing his scheme. Consuela kissed him and then got to work packing her gear.

Slocum walked into the jail and found Marshal Atkinson sitting behind his desk with his hand on a shotgun. The old lawman looked gray with strain.

"You thinking on shooting me?" Slocum asked.

"I heard things," the marshal said.

"That Denham wanted to string up Don Rodrigo?"

"El Loco? Yeah, heard that. A cowboy over at the Hijinx said Luther was in town tryin' to recruit men to lynch him."

Slocum tried to figure out how likely Atkinson was to stop Duke Denham if the outlaw wanted to break a prisoner out of the dilapidated jailhouse. The answer wasn't too cheering.

"You need to rustle up those deputies that went with us when we tracked down Rodrigo."

"They ain't nowhere to be found," Atkinson said. "I got to think hard on this." He fingered his shotgun, then pushed it away. Slocum took that as the answer to what the marshal would do if faced with a mob. Denham heading the mob would be even worse.

"Do your duty," Slocum said. "If Denham shows up, arrest him. You ought to throw Luther into the hoosegow, too, since he's one of the gang that tried to rob the stage twice."

"But they never succeeded."

"Because I shot holes in them when they tried," Slocum

said, working to hold down his anger. "In case you forgot, Don Rodrigo never held up the stage either."

"Then there's no reason to arrest Denham if he never robbed your stagecoach."

"Let El Loco go. I'll see that he doesn't get in your hair again."

"Cain't do that, Slocum. You know the reason."

"The town wants a marshal who can keep the peace, and you see Don Rodrigo as an easy way to show them you still have the sand for it."

"Watch what you say, boy." Atkinson reached for the shotgun again, but froze when he saw the steel in Slocum's eyes.

"Don't let a lynch mob take your prisoner," Slocum said. "You want the entire town to think they made a mistake paying you your salary, that's the way to do it. Protect anyone in your custody, even if it is a crazy Mexican."

"Close the door behind you when you leave, Slocum." Marshal Atkinson picked up his double-barreled shotgun and put his finger on the triggers.

Slocum resisted the urge to slam the door as he left. Instead, he pulled it shut gently behind him, came to a decision that he knew was probably wrong, and immediately walked to the rear of the jailhouse. He had seen the obvious flaws inside the cell. The wall where he had seen bricks coming loose afforded a quick entry inside, but he didn't pay a whole lot of attention to that. It would take too long and be too noisy.

He found a horse in the Butterfield corral, saddled, and went directly to the corral behind the jail where Rodrigo's horse nervously pawed the ground. Finding the tack was easy enough. Marshal Atkinson had simply dumped the saddle and bridle on the ground. Tying a rope around the saddle horn, Slocum led Don Rodrigo's horse to the barred jail window. A quick loop around the bars and a swat on the horse's rump pulled the iron bars out amid a cloud of dust and a loud crash.

"What is this?" Don Rodrigo looked up from inside the cell. Slocum said nothing. He reached in, grabbed a handful of shirt, and pulled. His horse backed away, giving Slocum the power to pull El Loco from the jail cell.

"Get on your horse," Slocum ordered. "Do it now. I'm taking you to your sister."

"Consuela? Why is she here? Where?"

"Get on," Slocum said, "or I'll hog-tie you and let your horse drag you."

"Do you know who I am? I am—" Don Rodrigo pulled himself up to his full height and struck a pose. Slocum trotted over, grabbed the small man again, and yanked him off his feet. It took a few seconds, but Slocum got him on his horse.

"I would see my sister," Don Rodrigo said haughtily. "I have matters to discuss with her. Important matters."

Slocum used a length of rope to lash the Mexican's horse to a gallop. He followed, wondering if this was going to get him into a world of trouble and if he should just keep riding. Being wanted for horse thieving was the least of his worries as long as he had to nursemaid Don Rodrigo de la Madrid y Garza.

5

"Oh, Rodrigo, you're safe." Consuela threw her arms around the shorter man and obviously embarrassed him. He tried to disengage from her arms, but couldn't. It was plenty different, but Slocum wouldn't want to push Consuela away had he been in Rodrigo's shabby boots.

"We've got to ride," Slocum said. "Get him across the Rio Grande into Mexico and you're both safe."

Consuela looked at him, eyes wide. She took a deep breath and then said, "How can I thank you, John? You have saved his life."

"Might have done more than that," he said. He saw the darkness come to Consuela when he said that. They both thought on what Duke Denham would do to the woman if he found her again. Slocum wanted to avoid it for Consuela's sake and to save himself the need of finding Denham and killing him like a rabid dog.

"Will you ride with us to the river?"

Slocum hesitated. He wanted to return the horse to the corral before Rasumussen noticed it was missing. For whatever reason, he wanted to keep his job as guard on the Butterfield stagecoaches a little while longer. The pay was scant, but the promise of actually being given a horse of his own for his work in only a week appealed to him. The one he rode now would do fine. She was a strong mare and able to gallop along for a couple miles without collapsing under him.

"Until we see the river. I want to make certain the marshal didn't fire up a posse to come after us." Slocum knew the chance of that was small. For all the noise he had made breaking Don Rodrigo out of jail, Slocum doubted the marshal was likely to come after them. Atkinson might make up a tall tale about a hundred men all armed with Gatling guns coming to spirit the prisoner away. Slocum didn't care much about what Atkinson had to do to soothe his own conscience and keep his job. What worried him more was Luther or another of Denham's gang learning that Rodrigo was gone.

Duke Denham had a yen for Consuela, and capturing her brother would go a ways toward giving him power over her. He might rape her, but keeping her around would be too dangerous. If he held her brother prisoner and threatened to kill Don Rodrigo, Consuela might be a more willing bed partner.

Slocum knew her well enough to realize Duke Denham would be wrong. Consuela would kill Denham, kill anyone holding her brother captive, and then proceed to do what she could to kill the entire gang. She would probably fail and die, along with her brother, but she would take a few of the outlaws with her before she checked out.

"I do not want to return to Mexico," Don Rodrigo said. "This is a fine land. I would move my hacienda here and rule all of West Texas!" He made a grand gesture that both Consuela and Slocum ignored.

"*Por favor, mi hermano*. We return home for the moment."

With Don Rodrigo riding all about, making strange noises and erratically dipping and dodging things that were unseen by either his sister or Slocum, they rode toward the border separating the countries. Slocum heard the roar of the Rio Grande before he saw the deep canyon it cut through the hills.

"We're here," he said. The spray from the river rose and felt like ice on his face. "Can you make it across?"

"We have both done so many times," Consuela said sadly. "Too many times for poor Rodrigo." She looked at him. The starlight caught her dark eyes and turned them silver. "Why do you do this for him? All the others laugh at him and blame him for any theft."

Slocum didn't have a good answer for her. He could ignore only so much casual cruelty and injustice directed at those who could not defend themselves. Perhaps Don Rodrigo amused him with his clownish antics, or Slocum might just feel sorry for the man. Either of those was not the noble reason Consuela sought.

"Go on, get across. It'll be dawn in an hour. You'll want to be far away into Mexico by then."

"Come into Mexico when you can. I'll be glad to see you." She left no question in Slocum's mind what she meant about being glad to see him again.

"Stranger things have happened. It's been a while since I rode south of the border." He didn't bother telling her that the *federales* might still be hunting for him after the dustup he had found himself caught in at the time. Two men had died and much silver had disappeared, none of which Slocum had been responsible for. That hadn't mattered to the Mexico authorities since he was a gringo and on the wrong side of the border.

Consuela leaned far out of the saddle and gave him a light kiss that didn't satisfy either of them. She drew back, touched her lips, then turned and rode down the steep slope toward the river, where Don Rodrigo already allowed his horse to drink. Slocum waited until both were safely across the rapidly running Rio Grande before turning his own pony's face back toward Eagle Pass.

Dawn awakened on the eastern plains, and soon the rising

sun forced Slocum to pull his hat brim down to shade his eyes. As he rode, he thought on Consuela and Don Rodrigo and everything that had happened to him in the past few weeks. He sat straighter in the saddle when he heard a horse off to his right. Slocum turned in time to see the rider lifting a rifle to his shoulder.

Slocum put his spurs to the mare's flanks and rocketed off. The rifle report came a fraction of a second after he heard the whine of the bullet cutting through the air. He rode into a ravine and then worked his way around, cutting to a sandy patch, and finally reaching a rise where he could get a good look at the sniper. As his horse struggled up the slope, he pulled his Winchester from its sheath. There was no reason the man trying to gun him down had to have all the fun.

As he topped the rise, Slocum got a better look at the sniper.

"Die, Luther," Slocum said as he lifted his rifle to firing position. Just as he squeezed the trigger, the outlaw spotted him and moved. From the way Luther jumped, Slocum knew his slug had come close—but he had not even winged the outlaw. Luther vanished in a cloud of dust. Slocum chose not to track him down, though that time would come eventually. He realized one reason he had not gone with Consuela into Mexico was the need to even the score with Luther and Duke Denham. They were giving outlawry a bad name.

He trotted back into Eagle Pass just as Jonah Rasumussen came from the depot. The man looked frustrated, so Slocum tried to avoid him and the inevitable questions about where he had ridden on one of the Butterfield horses.

"Slocum! Get your ass over here. Now!"

Slocum rode to the station agent and dismounted. He wiped dust from his cheeks.

"Find it?"

Slocum didn't have any idea what Rasumussen was

talking about, so he countered with, "One of Denham's gang shot at me. I tried to return the favor but I missed."

"Damnation, this is getting serious." Rasumussen paced back and forth and then stopped, facing Slocum. "Get another horse. That one's about wore out. Take care and if you find one of those sons of bitches, you shoot first. You have official Butterfield Stagecoach Company authorization."

Slocum nodded. He led the mare around to the corral where Smitty worked to feed the horses penned there.

"Morning," Slocum said. "Rasumussen wants me to get another horse and get back out."

"Did you find the break in the wire?" Smitty asked. He shook his head sadly. "Rasumussen is as nervy as a broken tooth over not being able to get instructions from San Antonio. I declare, that man lives by his damn telegraphed orders. It's a wonder he has pants on since they couldn't send him orders to dress."

Smitty continued feeding the horses as Slocum picked another. He saddled and led it from the corral.

"You think the telegraph's down south of town?"

"Sure as hell doesn't matter if it's down to the north. Rasumussen wants to stay in touch with the home office, not anyone to the north."

"Did he want me to fix it if I find the break? I'll need some wire and pliers."

"All he said to me that he wanted was for you to find the break. I reckon he'll send the Western Union crew out right away. Those lazy bastards will sit on their cracker asses until you kick 'em hard enough to fix their own telegraph wires."

Slocum knew all he needed. He mounted and rode to the wire road. It diverged from the main road less than a hundred yards outside Eagle Pass. He angled away and followed the telegraph poles, keeping the sun glinting off the wires above his head. There were any number of reasons the telegraph line might be out. The far end of the line might have experienced problems. Slocum had seen lead-acid batteries explode in the heat. Wind might have loosened an insulator or pulled down the line. The other reason the telegraph wasn't working worried him a mite more. The Apaches were noted for cutting the wires to keep the cavalry from learning where they were headed.

Slocum craned his neck and made sure the sun reflected off the wire. If Apaches had cut the line, they might have tied the severed ends together with rawhide. That prevented the signal from reaching its destination and made it more difficult for a lineman to find the spot to repair it.

By midday, he had found the break in the line and decided to rest. The sun beat down savagely and turned him as weak as a newborn kitten. He sat in the dubious shade of a telegraph pole while he chewed on a piece of jerky that wasn't too maggot-infested and sipped water from his canteen. The last of the jerky had settled in his belly when he heard horses coming closer.

He stood and shielded his eyes against the glaring sun. He grabbed his rifle and levered a round in when he saw three Apaches trotting along the wire road. Rather than start the shooting, he hoped they would veer away and not see him at all. Less than a minute after this fantasy had built in his head, he knew it would never happen. The leader pointed ahead, let out a war whoop, and came galloping forward.

Slocum squeezed off a shot and missed. He fired again, and then the Apache warrior was on top of him. The brave swung a war club and grazed the side of Slocum's head, sending him tumbling to the ground. The blow had missed crushing his skull, but had hit hard enough to daze him. He groped around for his rifle, but couldn't find it. Then he had other things to worry over. The Apache dived from horseback and crashed into him, knocking him flat on the ground.

Knowing his life would be forfeit if he didn't get out

from under the wiry brave, Slocum forced his left shoulder up, dropped, and put all his strength into tossing the Apache off to the right. He unbalanced the warrior, but did not completely unseat him. Slocum drew up his right knee and slammed it into the brave's back, keeping him from getting his knees onto Slocum's shoulders and effectively pinning him.

More than annoying his opponent, Slocum wanted his right boot up where he could grab for it. His fingers closed on the hilt of his knife. He slid it free of the boot and then drew it in what had to be an agonizing line across the Apache's back. The Indian screeched in pain and turned. This was all Slocum needed to heave again and drive the warrior to the hard ground. He used his knife, sliding it under the Apache's ribs and up into a throbbing heart. The Indian died instantly.

Slocum looked up and saw he had even worse trouble to face. He had a knife in his hand. The two Indians riding with the slain one both had their rifles trained on him. Even if he had his own rifle cocked and aimed, he could never have killed two of them before one shot him. Refusing to give in easily, Slocum threw his knife at the nearest brave. It tumbled hilt over point, but did not stick in flesh. The Indian brushed it away contemptuously, and raised his rifle as he barked out something to his companion.

Slocum guessed the warrior wanted this kill for himself. He went for his Colt Navy, but he was drawing against a man with a rifle already to fire.

The report sounded strange to his ears. Slocum hoped the Indian's rifle had misfired. He whipped out his six-shooter and fired twice—and his slugs drove through empty air. The Apache had already been shot from horseback.

Slocum turned his six-gun toward the remaining brave and emptied his Colt. The brave's horse reared and pawed at the air, preventing its rider from accurately firing. Slocum scooped up his rifle and fired. His aim was perfect. The warrior toppled to the ground, dead before he crashed into the dry West Texas desert.

"So, you now thank Don Rodrigo de la Madrid y Garza for his fine marksmanship?"

Slocum whirled around. Astride his horse, not ten yards off, sat Don Rodrigo. The man held a rifle in his hands. Smoke curled from the muzzle, showing who had drilled the Apache about to kill Slocum.

"How'd you get here?" Slocum looked at the three braves and decided they couldn't be any deader, then walked to Don Rodrigo. "Where's Consuela?"

"She is in Mexico where she belongs. Taming this wild land is a man's job. *My* job!" Rodrigo struck one of his poses, imitating European kings sitting for official portraits.

"I'm much obliged you decided to come back when you did," Slocum said, "but you shouldn't have come back. It's safer for you on the other side of the river."

"I will establish the finest hacienda in all of Texas here. You are my foreman."

"Don Rodrigo," Slocum began, but the vaquero rode off at a gallop, firing his rifle in the air as he went.

"Son of a bitch," Slocum grumbled. He took what he could off the dead Indians, then looked around for his horse. It had run off in the melee. A quick search showed the Apaches' horses were similarly missing. The only piece of luck he had was that his canteen had not been slung on his saddle—which was still on his horse somewhere in the desert.

He downed a mouthful, then went hunting for his horse. Even if it had galloped hard, it would slow and eventually halt. Tracking in the desert was difficult, but he had a good idea what direction the animal had gone. It took the better part of an hour to find the horse nibbling at beans from a mesquite bush.

It was after dark when Slocum rode back into Eagle Pass. His horse staggered beneath him, and Slocum felt hardly better. He went directly to the Butterfield corral and tended to the horse, making sure it had water, food, and then some more water. Slocum's belly growled from lack of food, but his thirst, like that of his horse, was paramount. He poked his head into the Butterfield office, looking for Rasumussen to report what he had found, but the station agent was nowhere to be seen. That suited Slocum just fine. The town was strangely quiet, but Slocum hardly noticed as he pushed his way into the Hijinx Saloon.

Again, the quiet hardly made an impression on him as he went to the bar and leaned heavily against it.

"Beer," he said. "As cold as you can make it."

"Thought you'd be out with the rest of 'em, Slocum," the barkeep said. He worked a mug around in a small bucket of snow, left some in the mug, and filled it with frothy beer.

Slocum downed the cool beer and felt better as it first cooled him and then warmed his belly. The aches began to fade and he felt almost human.

"Got anything to eat left from lunch?"

"Some," the barkeep said, rummaging about under the bar. He pulled out a plate of beef in congealed grease and what remained of a loaf of bread. To Slocum, it looked like a banquet. When he finished eating, he got another beer and decided life wasn't so bad after all.

"So where'd you say everybody was?" Slocum finally asked. The barkeep looked strangely reluctant to answer.

The barkeep backed off a ways and found a spot at the end of the bar.

"Thought you knew."

"I just rode in from finding the spot along the telegraph line where the wire came down. Ran into Apache raiders, too." Before he could even mention Don Rodrigo's help getting him out of a jam, the barkeep blurted out the news.

"He shot a man in the back."

Slocum looked at the bartender. He didn't understand what the man meant.

"Who?"

"Just some cowboy from the J-Bar-J. Never heard his name, but he wasn't wearin' a hogleg. He just upped and shot him in the back."

"Who are you talking about?"

"El Loco. He murdered a man."

"But he—" Slocum clamped his mouth shut. Don Rodrigo might have ridden directly to Eagle Pass after saving Slocum's hide and gotten into a fight. It was unlikely, but Slocum had spent most of the afternoon tracking down his wayward horse, and then the heat had hammered him into a slow return to town.

Slocum doubted Rodrigo had made it back to town that fast, but he couldn't shake the uneasy feeling that it was possible. With El Loco, any crazy behavior was possible.

6

"I declare, the sun gets hotter ever' single day," Smitty complained. He mopped the flood of sweat pouring into his eyes with one hand while expertly keeping the reins in the other. The team wasn't feeling too frisky today, and he had no trouble with them.

Slocum understood that. Nothing the last couple days had been right. He had almost been killed by Indians the day before and then rescued by Don Rodrigo, who was being sought by then marshal and damned near everyone in Eagle Pass for killing a cowboy. Slocum puzzled over how Rodrigo could have reached town in time to do the killing, but it was barely possible. The evidence against him was flimsy since the two citizens who accused El Loco were more drunk than sober. Slocum had wanted to find the Mexican vaquero and find out the best he could what the real situation was, but he'd run into a brick wall looking for Don Rodrigo.

If that wasn't enough, Rasumussen was nervous about a missing freight shipment, and had sent the stage out a day early because he had six passengers wanting to reach points north. From what Slocum could tell, the men were connected with the Department of the Interior and had something to do with policy about Indians and their reservations. They had spent a month in San Antonio, and were now on an inspection tour that took them north to Mesilla and from there to several Apache reservations. He did not envy the men either the trip or their job.

"Not much farther till the way station," Slocum said.

"I hope that old fool Jesse's got a rested team waitin' for us," Smitty said. "He's been gettin' lazier by the day and claimin' he can't find horses. I think he's been eatin' 'em, if you ask me."

"He's that hungry?"

"You think Butterfield pays you shit? He gets even less for twice the work." Smitty stood and peered into the hazy distance. "We're not a mile out. Time to find out if we're movin' on right away or spendin' time whilst he finds six nags to hitch up."

Slocum knew that their passengers were in a hurry, but he hoped that Jesse took his time. Slocum's butt ached from being bounced around on the hardwood seat, his arms and back hurt after the ride yesterday, and mostly he felt hollow inside. After all the trouble he had gone to on Don Rodrigo's behalf, the man had sneaked back across the Rio Grande just to do some killing. Shooting the Apaches threatening Slocum must have given him a taste for blood that he was too crazy to control.

Smitty used his whip to get the horses up the last steep incline to reach the way station, but Slocum looked out across the desert. A steady wind blew today, sucking the moisture from a soul's body, but it also kicked up dust and obscured the horizon. In spite of the shifting brown cloud whipping across the land, he thought he spied a rider. Slocum wiped the grit from his face, squinted, and cupped his hand to better shield his eyes. The stagecoach bounced about too much for him to find the spot where he had seen the rider.

In a strange, fanciful way, he thought it might be Don Rodrigo. If it was, Slocum wouldn't be able to do anything about it. He felt torn. Don Rodrigo had saved his life, but he had also killed another man, by all accounts an unarmed cowboy whose only crime had been being in the Mexican's gunsight. If Slocum caught him, he wasn't sure what he would do. Before, it had been easy to put him in Consuela's care and spirit the pair of them across the Rio Grande. But now? Slocum hoped he would not have to decide what to do with the man who had saved his life.

"All out. Stretch your legs, get some water. We won't be here long," Smitty yelled. He launched himself into the air and landed hard on the ground. The team shied a little, but the driver soothed them as he moved forward to unhitch the leads.

Slocum climbed down more slowly. The six passengers flopped out of the furnacelike compartment, staggered about until they got their balance back after being tossed around inside the stagecoach, and looked around skeptically.

"Can we get a drink here?" one asked Slocum.

"Unless Jesse's got a bottle hid away, only water," Slocum said.

The man grumbled, but the other five were content to get even this small liquid gift. They went into the tumbledown shack where Jesse lived. Slocum went around to help Smitty swap out the team. The driver already had the last pair unhitched, and Slocum was about to lead them to the corral when he stopped and frowned. Something wasn't right.

He checked the horses and wondered at how skittish they had become. With deft hands, he pulled them away from the tongue and led them toward the corral, where one reared and pawed the air.

Slocum hesitated. He had been leading the horses into the wind. That meant that some smell caught on the brisk, hot breeze had spooked them.

"Smitty, we've got trouble coming," he yelled. He closed

the gate behind the horses. "Grab a shotgun, just to be sure."

"Them bureaucrats got any guns?" The driver ran back to the stagecoach and climbed to the box to grab his sawed-off scattergun. It lacked range, but within five yards it was as deadly as any weapon.

"Hideout guns maybe," Slocum said. "I didn't see that any of them carried six-shooters."

Smitty stood beside him, peering into the dust cloud blowing toward them.

"That'd hide a whole damn army, wouldn't it?"

Slocum didn't answer. He was too busy getting his Winchester to his shoulder and shooting at the Apache racing out of the cover of the windstorm. His bullet went high, but caused the Indian to veer away. Behind him came three more. Then another six.

"Jesus," muttered Smitty. "We got ourselves caught in front of a full-sized war party."

Slocum emptied his rifle and backed toward the way station. The walls were paper thin and would hardly stop an arrow, much less a bullet. It wouldn't take the war chief leading the Apaches but an instant to figure out how easy it would be to burn them out. Why hadn't the Butterfield Stage Company built Jesse a real adobe with thick mud walls? It would have kept him cooler in the summer heat and stopped even an Apache bullet.

"What's going on? Why're you shooting?" one of the passengers asked.

"If you got a piece, get to usin' it," Smitty said. "We're up to our asses in Apache raiders." He spun and looked at the far side of the way station. The driver pulled up his shotgun and fired both barrels, taking an Apache off his horse to flop about in the dust.

Slocum didn't bother trying to reload his rifle. He drew his six-gun. Unfortunately, the Indians galloping toward him were all in range. He wished they had all been too far away for easy shooting—but that wasn't to be. Firing methodically, he shot one and caused the others to break off their attack.

"They're not out for personal glory," Slocum said, crowding the passengers back into the way station. "They aren't intent on fighting as much as bottling us up."

"You mean they'd keep attacking even if you were firing?" asked a passenger.

"They're after something more than killing us, though doing that wouldn't make them lose any sleep," Slocum said.

"The horses! That's what them red sonsabitches want!" The station agent grabbed his rifle and ran across the single room to a loophole cut in the back wall. He poked his rifle through and started firing. "I was right. Them varmints're stealin' the horses."

"If they take the horses, will they let us go?"

Slocum looked at the passenger. He had been the one inquiring after a snort of whiskey. Nothing in his tone made him sound the least bit frightened. He simply asked for information to act on.

"You ever fire a rifle?" Slocum asked.

"Third Massachusetts Volunteers," the man said. Slocum tossed him his rifle and pointed to a table where a couple boxes of cartridges had been spilled.

"Make every shot count."

"They want our scalps?"

"They got our horses, that's for certain sure," Jesse moaned.

"Butterfield won't take their price out of your salary," Smitty said. "Rasumussen might be a bastard, but he knows what we face out here."

"How we gonna get away from them without horses?" Jesse fired faster now. Slocum couldn't see if he had good targets or simply filled the air with lead, hoping volume would drive off the Apaches.

"They might let us be," Smitty said. He stood in the doorway, then bolted outside and discharged both barrels of his shotgun again. Slocum followed, his Colt Navy ready.

"Where are you going?" Slocum shouted. The driver dodged and weaved to avoid both Apache arrows and bullets as he headed for the stagecoach.

"Got more ammo in the back of the stage," he said. "We're gonna need all we can get." The words hardly escaped his lips when he vented an earsplitting shriek of pure agony.

"Damn," Slocum muttered. He sucked in his breath, then ran after Smitty. The driver thrashed around on the ground beside the stage, an arrow pinning his leg to the ground. A huge red stain spread on his pants leg just above his boot.

"Don't thrash about so much," Slocum said. "You look like a trout tossed onto the bank of some mountain stream."

"Quit tryin' to make me feel better, Slocum. Get the ammo. I got dang near a case of rifle rounds in the boot."

Slocum dropped his six-shooter into the driver's trembling hands. Smitty fired it almost instantly. The hot lead sang past Slocum's head. From the corner of his eye he saw a mounted brave recoil. Smitty's aim was good. Slocum ripped open the canvas flap and pawed through the luggage stored in the boot until he found a wood box. Clawing at it, he ripped off the lid and saw ten boxes of rifle cartridges inside.

"You got any more shotgun shells back here?" Slocum called. He had to yell over the report of his Colt Navy.

"Nope, just ammo for the rifle."

Slocum heaved the box out and held it under his left arm. He ran back to Smitty, gripped the arrow still holding the man to the ground, broke off the shaft, and yanked hard on the leg so that it slid free. The driver let out a groan and sagged back.

"Don't pass out on me," Slocum said. He took the pistol

from Smitty's limp fingers and holstered it. Then he grabbed the man's leather vest and started dragging him toward the dubious safety of the way station. A few bullets tore past, but they weren't close enough to make Slocum duck. When he got to the door, a couple of the passengers got hold of Smitty and pulled him inside. Slocum swung through the door and put the box of cartridges on the table. The rounds that had been there when he and Smitty had gone outside were all gone. Jesse was still firing up a storm.

"Slow down, old man," Slocum yelled. "You'll melt your barrel."

"Won't matter if they scalp the lot of us," Jesse said.

"I tried to tell him," the passenger with Slocum's rifle said. "He wouldn't listen."

Slocum didn't try to explain that the station agent probably understood the threat they faced better than anyone else. He lived here alone and either went crazy fearing for his life whenever he saw a rider, or came to grips with what the real dangers were.

"You want this back?" the passenger with the rifle asked.

"Let's see how good the Federals trained their soldiers," Slocum said.

The passenger looked sharply at Slocum, then said, "The war's over."

"That war. We got ourselves a brand-new one, compliments of Victorio and his kin." Slocum reloaded his six-gun, then knelt beside Smitty. The man was pale but alert.

"Wish I had more shells for that blunderbuss of mine," said Smitty.

"It's outside," Slocum said. "It wouldn't do us much good anyway. If they get close enough for a shotgun, we're pretty much dead."

"I was 'fraid you'd say somethin' like that. We don't have any more guns?"

"Two rifles and my six-shooter," Slocum said. "But

there's plenty of ammunition for the rifles." He clapped Smitty on the shoulder. "You rest up. We'll have them run off in a while."

"They ain't turnin' tail and runnin'," Jesse called. "They got the horses already. Not sure what more they want."

"Water," said the passenger. "The cavalry is tightening a noose around them by staking out their watering holes."

"Cut the Apaches off from their water and they'll go away? Is that the plan?" Slocum asked.

"Kill them when they come to the water holes," the man said. "*That* is the plan."

"Sounds like a damn good plan, if only it'd work," Jesse said.

"It must be working," Slocum said. "Like you said, they want more than the horses. They want our water."

"This is the only sweet water spring between here and Eagle Pass," Jesse said. "Hardly gives enough in a day to water the horses, but enough."

"That's what they want," Slocum said. He pressed his face against the plank wall and got a view of the well not twenty feet away. "If we can keep them from the water, they'll have to give up and go away."

"They'll be willing to lay siege," Jesse said.

"Not if they're runnin' shy o' water," Smitty said. "Might be we can poison the well."

"No!" Jesse was as aggrieved at this notion as any man could be. "That's my water, damn your eyes. I have to live here. Without the water, there's no way station and I don't make a thin dime."

"Find somethin' else to do," Smitty said.

Slocum wanted to tell the driver to pipe down. His face was as white as bleached muslin and his hands shook something fierce. For such a minor wound, that arrow had done quite a job on him. Slocum wondered if the Apaches had taken to poisoning their arrowheads. He wouldn't put it past them to drop a little scorpion venom on the edges.

"They won't fight longer than a day," the passenger with Slocum's rifle said. "The cavalry has to be hot on their trail. If they waste too much time in any single place, they'll have quite a fight on their hands."

"So where're them black 'uns?" grumbled Jesse.

"It won't be dark for another couple hours," Slocum said. "The Apaches will fight until then. We'll have the night to rest up."

"Why's that?"

Slocum wasn't sure which of the other passengers asked, but he thought it was a stupid question from a man who would determine the fate of all the Apaches. The question showed he didn't know very much about the people he planned to bottle up on worthless land far from their traditional hunting range.

"They are deathly afraid of rattlesnakes," said the man with the rifle.

Slocum was glad someone in the government commission sent out to oversee the savages knew something about them.

"If we can hold them off, keep them away from the well until sundown, I can go fetch some water for us," Slocum said. He saw that the bucket Jesse kept drinking water in was almost empty. They would get powerful thirsty long before the sun dropped behind the far-off Davis Mountains.

"They might be too desperate for that," Smitty said. He sat up, eyes bright and looking flushed. "We got to get out of here."

"Settle down, son," Jesse said. "Your guard's got the right idea. We keep those redskins 'way from the water and they'll give up. I can't see 'em hangin' 'round till morning."

Jesse ducked as a bullet tore through the wall just above his head. He grumbled and went back to his loophole to take a few quick shots in the direction of the corral.

Slocum chanced a look outside, judged how far it was to

the well, and knew he could get there, pull up some water, and return in less than two minutes. Under the cover of darkness, it wouldn't be difficult since the Apaches would have to ride up to get at him. There wasn't anywhere nearby for them to take cover.

Unless . . .

"Any way to get onto the roof from inside here?" Slocum asked.

Jesse cast a puzzled look over his shoulder at Slocum.

"What you got in mind?"

"I don't want one of them on the roof when I go for the water," Slocum said.

"Ain't any way up there 'less you got a ladder outside. No reason to get onto the roof from inside. Damn thing leaks bad enough whenever it decides to rain, which ain't often enough." The way station agent went back to his vigil, looking for Apache targets.

"You want me to go up and cover you when you go for the water?" asked the passenger Slocum suspected was the leader of the commission. "Or would you rather go up and let me fetch the water?"

"It's going to be dangerous, no matter where you are," Slocum pointed out.

The man shrugged. It didn't matter much to him.

"Massachusetts Volunteers?" Slocum asked. This startled the man. He looked harder at Slocum. "Think we ever faced each other on the battlefield?" Slocum asked.

"Depends on where you fought," the man said.

"Don't go tearin' open old wounds," Jesse said. "It's gettin' toward dusk now. What you gonna do, Slocum? Head out for water now or wait to draw 'em in?"

Slocum considered the need for a sharpshooter on the roof. He took a quick look around again and decided there wasn't any call for anyone to risk getting onto the roof to lay down covering fire. The Apaches had to know something would happen when the sun went down. While they were afraid of snakes and went to ground at night, if their lives depended on a nighttime fight, they'd do it.

"They're just beyond the corral," Jesse reported. "Looks like they're thinkin' on an assault 'fore it gets too dark."

"We got to get away," Smitty said. "They'll keep us penned up in here if we don't get help. You said there was a cavalry troop prowlin' about, lookin' for 'em?"

"Somewhere," the passenger said. "I have no idea where they are patrolling, though."

"We got to get to 'em."

"You shut yer tater trap," Jesse said to Smitty. "You drink up the rest of the water. A fever's makin' you talk crazy."

"I know what I'm sayin'," Smitty said. Slocum doubted it, though. He had ridden with the driver long enough to know he tended toward taciturn. If two words would do, Smitty pared it down to one.

Slocum made sure Smitty drank the last of the water. The man's bright eyes still spoke to the fever gripping his brain, but the flush was gone now and he seemed stronger.

"All right," Slocum said. "Let's see if we can't decoy some of them out. You plug as many as you can, Jesse. You, too," he said to the passenger.

Slocum grabbed the bucket, took a deep breath, then ran hard for the well. When he was halfway there, the Apaches had not noticed him, but by the time he reached the low rock wall, their lead sailing through the air kept him low. He heard return fire from the way station. Taking the rope draped over the edge of the well, he tied the bucket to it and tossed it down. The splash reassured him. He began drawing the bucket back, trying not to worry too much about the occasional expertly shot arrow that arched upward and landed beside him. He didn't give the Apaches a direct shot, so they tried lobbing their arrows at him.

Grunting, he pulled the bucket over the wall and gripped its rope handle. Slocum dashed back to the cabin and slid inside, panting from the exertion.

"Got it. How many of them did you kill?" he asked.

Only silence greeted him. He looked around, but Jesse's dour expression alerted him to what was wrong.

"Where's Smitty?"

"The damn fool took it into his head to get help, I reckon," Jesse said. "Never saw him go out, but I did see him out by the corral."

Slocum forced Jesse aside and peered out the loophole. In the light of the setting sun he saw two braves dragging an unconscious man between them. Smitty had been captured.

7

"He's a goner. You know what Apaches do to their captives," Jesse said. He shook his head sadly and helped himself to a dipper of water. "Didn't think Smitty was out of his head, but seems I was wrong."

"They won't take him far," Slocum said. "They want the water. If we watch for a brave sneaking in, we can keep them at bay."

"They know what we think about saving friends' lives," the passenger said. "They might try to swap Smitty for water. What do we do then? Let him be tortured to death or give them what they want?"

"They'll kill us all," Slocum said. "They have no reason to let us live once they get the water." His mind raced. The possibilities were all bad ones, but one scheme kept coming back to Slocum. It was dangerous, but simply sitting and taking potshots at any Apache getting close to the water was dangerous, too. It wouldn't be long before the Indians decided to fire a few flaming arrows into the way station to drive out anyone foolish enough to oppose them.

"We can't just let them torture him," protested another of the passengers. He looked frightened and turned away when everyone stared at him.

"You going out to rescue the driver, Lamar?" The commission member Slocum had decided was in charge had leveled the question.

"It's not his place," Slocum said. "You're passengers and you paid the Butterfield Company to get you safely to your destination." He spun the cylinder in his six-shooter, then rammed it back into his holster. Gunfire was less likely to succeed than using the knife sheathed in the top of his boot. "Don't be too quick to shoot anyone coming back toward the well," Slocum said. He opened the door, but Jesse grabbed his arm to stop him.

"You're fixin' to get yourself killed."

"He's a friend," Slocum said. He pulled away, crouched down, and then wiggled through the dust outside the way station until he got to the far side where he could get a better view of the corral and desert beyond. Smoke rising high into the evening sky from a fire hidden behind a sandy rise told him where the Apaches had camped. It also told him where they had laid a trap for the unwary.

His tactic had been to take out the Indians one at a time as they tried to reach the well. They were no fools. They were turning the tables by luring out rescuers, one by one, to save Smitty. Attrition had worked during the war, with one side grinding down the other soldier by soldier. That tactic worked even better here where neither side could count on reinforcements arriving. If the Apaches killed enough men in the way station, the survivors might be gulled into surrendering—and dying without further fighting.

Slocum moved as quietly as he could away from the way station, heading parallel to the road for several hundred yards before circling around to approach the Apache camp from the flank. Even so, he almost missed a sentry hunkered down by a mesquite tree. If it hadn't been for the man slapping at a bug on his neck, Slocum might have missed him—and died.

As silent as the evening breeze, Slocum slipped around behind the Indian. The mesquite bush between them proved a problem. The sharp, long thorns would cut him to bloody strips if he tried to push through to get to the Apache. Slocum drew his knife, edged to one side, and then let out a hiss as close to that of a rattler as he could make it.

The Apache shot to his feet, stumbled, and died in a flash. Slocum surged forward and caught the frightened guard under the ribs with his knife. His forearm corded with muscles as he applied all his strength to drive the blade higher into the Apache's gut until the brave's spastic kicking ceased.

Slocum lowered the body to the ground, cleaned the knife by plunging it into the dry ground, and took the Indian's rifle. He sat for a minute to get his bearings and gather his wits about him. The Apaches were more spooked than he had thought if they had put a sentry this far from camp.

Or were they being cautious? A third possibility seemed more likely to him. The fire had been built to draw attention from those in the way station, but the actual camp wasn't too far off. Acting on this guess, Slocum made his way another twenty yards and discovered he was right.

They had not built a fire here, but eight Apaches crowded close together for warmth. To one side, stretched out spread-eagle on the ground, lay a dim shape that had to be Smitty. Slocum waited for a moan or some twitch that showed the driver was still alive, but nothing came to reassure him his mission was likely to be successful. For all he knew, Smitty was already dead.

If there were eight Apaches here, that meant at least that number at the trap and scattered around as sentries. He was glad that the Apaches hated dogs. He was upwind from the cold camp and would have alerted any animal with a sensitive nose.

Moving slowly and carefully, Slocum came within a dozen paces of where Smitty lay on his back. Belly down,

Slocum watched for more than ten minutes for some sign of life. When he finally saw it in the prisoner's feeble twitching, he almost got caught.

Smitty moaned and attracted the attention of a guard Slocum had not seen. The sentry came from the shadows and towered over his captive. He uttered something obscene in Apache and kicked Smitty hard in the ribs. The prisoner let out a low moan that convinced Slocum he was far from dead. A stream of curses followed the moan, only to have them cut off by another hard kick to the ribs. The guard walked away.

Slocum had no plan. He simply reacted. His knife came out and a short run brought him up behind the retreating guard. Slocum caught the Apache under the chin and snapped his head back at the same time he cut his throat. The warrior died swiftly, but made some small sounds that attracted unwanted attention from the camp.

"Lemme go!" shrieked Smitty. "You bastards! You can't do this to me!"

Slocum eased the dead guard to the ground and returned to the captive driver.

"That enough caterwaulin'?" Smitty asked.

Slocum nodded once, then began slicing the rawhide strips binding Smitty's wrists and ankles. The man tried to get up, but Slocum pushed him back to the ground and whispered, "Get circulation back before trying to walk."

Waiting a few minutes more was risky, but not as chancy as slipping away only to find that Smitty's legs gave way under him because of his ordeal.

"I'm ready, Slocum."

Slocum grabbed the man's wrist and felt it. The flesh was still cold, but the fingers balled into a hard fist. Sensation had returned to his hands. Slocum nodded and then pressed the captured rifle into Smitty's hands.

"You up to using that?"

"I'm not as feverish as I was."

Slocum helped him up, wishing they had time to find Smitty's boots. His feet would be ground meat by the time they got back to the way station.

Slocum appreciated the way Smitty kept the sounds of his obvious agony down until they were well away from the Apaches. He pushed the man to the ground and whispered orders in his ear.

"Go on back to the station. It's that way, but you will avoid the Indians if you keep walking straight until you reach the road, then follow it back."

Smitty nodded, but when Slocum stood and started in another direction, he called, "Where you goin'?"

"To help convince them to give up."

"There's a couple dozen of the bastards," Smitty said. "I was outta my head thinkin' to get past that many of them to get some help."

"You're still burning up with fever," Slocum said. "You'll start doing dumb things again when the fear wears off. You had better be back at the way station when that happens. Besides, they can use the extra rifle. Now git!"

Slocum didn't wait to see if Smitty was heading in the right direction. He had heard a neighing horse not far off. The desperate plan that had come to him required him stealing those horses back from the Apaches.

There was some stirring in the Apache camp, but they stayed close and didn't come looking for him. Slocum hurried to where the Indians had staked out a dozen horses. He moved through the small herd, checking brands. All were Butterfield horses. Looping rope around their necks, he kept them in a long string, and only mounted the final one when he was sure the rest would follow. Bareback, he pressed his knees down hard to guide the lead horse he had chosen, using both hands on the ropes securing the rest. Slocum had barely ridden a dozen yards when a loud cry of anger rose from behind him. Another sentry had spotted him. He urged his horse to a trot and was almost unseated when the rest of his small herd balked.

Forcing his horse around in a tight circle, Slocum yanked on the ropes and got a few of the horses heading in the right direction. By now the guard's cries filled the still night. Barely had Slocum brought the horses to a walk when a bullet tore through the night. Then he had a stampede on his hands. He bent low as he rode, trying to keep up with the rest of the horses. He didn't try to guide them. It was enough that they ran away from the Apache camp.

After a mile, they began to tire. After two, they stumbled along. He tugged and jerked to get them in line again and under control. The horses were tuckered out and walked along only under the greatest urging, but he succeeded in getting them to the road. A quick look at the stars oriented him and he headed toward the way station.

To his relief, he found Smitty stumbling along when he estimated they were less than a quarter mile from rejoining the others.

"Climb on up and ride," Slocum said.

"Gonna fall off, the way I feel all dizzy and sick to my stomach," Smitty protested. In spite of this protest, he threw his arms around one horse's neck and crawled up. He kept his arms in a stranglehold on the strong neck and let Slocum lead him back to within a dozen yards of the way station.

"It's me, Slocum. I got Smitty!" Slocum worked to keep the horses in line until Jesse and the others recognized him.

"You got Injuns on your tail?"

"Don't think so, but I've got a dozen Butterfield horses with me."

"And Smitty?"

"I'm doin' just fine, Jesse," the driver croaked out. "You better have some water waitin' for me or I'll twist that scrawny neck of yours into a knot."

"Come on in, you ornery varmint," Jesse said.

Slocum saw the way station agent poking his head out the door. The rifle wasn't aimed at them, but could be if the need arose.

Slocum stepped down from the horse and lashed the ropes on the others around a post. If the horses spooked, they'd pull the post out and run off. He only needed them to stand easy for a little while.

"Didn't expect to ever see you again," the passenger said. "Surely never thought to see Smitty either."

"I'm tough," the young driver said. "And Slocum's got brass balls to saunter into an Apache camp the way he did."

"You think that's something," Slocum said, "so let me tell you how we're all going to get out of here."

At first, they all shook their heads and refused to believe he was serious. Little by little, he convinced them the Apaches would never leave on their own. They were too desperate for water and probably knew they outnumbered the men in the way station three to one.

"So let me get this right," Jesse said. "Waitin' fer the damn cavalry's not gonna get us out of this alive, so we pretend to be the cavalry?"

"Can you blow that bugle hanging over your fireplace?"

"I used to blow it for the First Austin Militia," Jesse said.

From the corner of his eye, Slocum saw how the passenger from Massachusetts shook his head sadly. Right now that war was a relic of history. They had to fight out a new war and were forced to be on the front line, whether they liked it or not.

"All you need to do is blow 'charge' and we're good as gold," Slocum said, knowing he was stretching the truth a considerable amount.

"I kin do that. I remember reveille, too."

Slocum thought for a moment, then smiled.

"Here's the plan. You blow reveille. The Apaches have to know what that sounds like. We're all mounted on the horses. You begin blowing the signal for us to charge, and we do. All the horses, creating as much noise as we can."

"And we ride straight into the Apaches? That's a good way of dying," the passenger said.

"Staying and doing nothing is even surer a way of ending up scalped. We've got rifles, we've got plenty of ammunition. We make them think they're up against a company of cavalry. All we have to do is scare them away. If we tried fighting them off the way we have been, we'd be in a world of trouble." Slocum looked around the circle of grim, unbelieving faces and knew they were likely to be in the same sorry place no matter what they did, but fighting and dying was a sight better than waiting for the Apaches to burn them out and shoot them down like frightened rabbits.

"When do we go?" Smitty came over and used Jesse for support. "I prob'ly lost my bonus for gettin' these gents to Fort Davis on time, but if I make up a few hours along the way, I'll feel better about it."

This produced a chuckle that grew into laughter bordering on the hysterical. Slocum let them get control of themselves again. This was better than outright refusal. His plan meant that all of them had to join in or none of them would survive.

"Just before sunrise," Slocum said. "That's when we go."

"Then it's 'bout time," Jesse said. "You been out gallivantin' 'round most of the night. I make sunrise only an hour off."

"Good," Slocum said. "If we attack while it's still dark, they're less likely to fight back and be more inclined to scatter. Whatever you do, don't pursue them if they run. Stay near their camp and let the horses kick up as much fuss as possible."

"Make 'em think there's more of us than there are," Smitty said.

Jesse took down the battered trumpet, licked his chapped lips, and put the mouthpiece to his lips. A sorry sound leaked out. He wiped his lips, looked sheepish, then gave a bigger toot that caused Slocum to jump.

"That's what we need. Everyone, get on a horse. If you've got a gun, get ready to use it when we ride close enough to the camp. Let's go."

Slocum didn't give them any time for second thoughts. He wasn't so sure this wasn't suicidal, but he saw no other way for at least some of them to get away alive. They might use the horses to ride off in the dark and might actually escape, but the Apaches were likely to come after them when they got their water. It never paid to leave behind witnesses who could tell the cavalry when and where they had attacked and how many were in the band of raiders.

"Been a spell since I rode bareback," Jesse said. "Sort of like bein' a kid again." He put the bugle to his lips and squealed out a passable reveille while the others mounted.

Slocum got them moving in the direction of the Apache camp, ignoring the one where a curl of smoke still rose. That had been a trap. He wanted to divide the war party in two if he could.

"Blow, Jesse, blow it now," he said.

The stationmaster reared back and uncorked the most nerve-shattering rendition of the command to charge that Slocum had ever heard. If he hadn't seen the ragtag band riding bareback, he would have thought the entire Tenth Cavalry was ready for battle.

"Charge!" Slocum yelled. At the top of his lungs, he drew on his experience as a captain in the Confederate Army and shouted commands as if he were leading a full company of troopers. For their part, the passengers and Smitty caused such a thunder of hooves, Slocum felt as if he did lead fifty men into battle.

He drew his six-shooter and began firing when he spotted the first Apache. The others behind him with their rifles opened up. Slocum shouted until he went hoarse and kept the attack moving forward.

To his amazement, the trick worked. The Apaches fought at a disadvantage in the darkness. They found their horses and raced off, leaving much of their gear behind. Slocum had to call out orders for Smitty and Jesse not to give chase. Like him, they had gotten wrapped up in the attack.

When they finally stopped and Slocum had a chance to look around, he saw his small group of intrepid cavalry had not sustained a single casualty. Three horses had run off, but this was a small price to pay for such a complete victory.

"Reckon this only leaves one question," Slocum said to Smitty.

"What's that?"

"Do we hitch up the team and go on to Fort Davis or return to Eagle Pass?"

Smitty laughed and Slocum knew the answer. They reached Fort Davis, their team almost exhausted, by nightfall.

8

Only four horses pulled the team as Slocum drove back into Eagle Pass. They had delivered their passengers just fine, but Smitty had weakened as they made their way back with nothing more than a couple canvas bags of mail from the fort. Slocum had watched the driver wobbling a mite; then Smitty had almost fallen out of the driver's box and under the stagecoach wheels.

When one horse died in harness after they had passed the way station, Smitty had dropped down to release its team-mate and had collapsed. The freed horse had bolted and disappeared into the desert. By the time Slocum reached Smitty, he was burning with fever again and muttering about Jonah Rasumussen taking the price of the horses out of his pay.

Slocum had loaded Smitty into the passenger compartment and taken the reins. Pulling the heavy coach was a chore for only four horses, but he was in no particular hurry. Better to return eventually than not at all. The stage rolled into Eagle Pass only a day late. The clank and rattle of the stagecoach caused men and women to come out and stare. More than one whispered behind his hand, starting a round of gossip as to why Slocum was driving.

He pulled up in front of the Butterfield depot and jumped down. As he wrestled open the door and pulled Smitty from inside, he yelled to the small crowd forming, "Fetch a doctor. Smitty's got a bad fever." Nobody moved. Slocum propped Smitty against a railing and turned to face them. His dark mood exploded into rage. "Get the doctor or I'll start shooting everyone still standing here." When he went for his six-shooter, the crowd scattered like roaches.

"No call for that, Slocum," Rasumussen said. The man came from inside the depot. Sweat beaded his forehead and his hands shook. He wiped at his mouth and then looked around nervously. "Come on inside. Need help with him?"

Slocum grunted as he half carried, half dragged Smitty into the dim, cool interior of the stagecoach depot. The driver moaned and weakly thrashed about as Slocum guided him to a bench. Smitty stretched out on it and immediately passed out.

"You got a story to tell, betcha," Rasumussen said.

"He needs a doctor."

"You scared somebody into fetching that drunken sot of a sawbones. Smitty'd be better off if the vet looked at him. Has a better bedside manner." Rasumussen opened a desk drawer and pulled out a pint bottle of whiskey. A full inch vanished before he passed it over to Slocum. The bitter taste made Slocum gag. He needed water more than he did rotgut right now. He took a second sip, draining almost as much as Rasumussen.

"Jesse's holding down the way station against Apaches. They had us penned up there. We scared them off, then went on to Fort Davis and dropped off the passengers." Slocum looked at Smitty. The man's breathing had turned shallow and ragged. His face had an unhealthy gray pallor to it, and he looked a dozen years older than he had before leaving for Fort Davis.

"We got the telegraph line fixed. You gave good instructions where to find the break. I been burning up the wire with telegrams to the home office in San Antone."

"Telling them what's happening isn't going to help us out here."

"It already has. They got word through to the army and we got a company of soldiers on the way here. You need to tell them about the Apaches so they can track them down better."

Slocum looked longingly at the whiskey bottle in Rasumussen's hands, but the station manager didn't offer another pull on it. All thought of liquor disappeared when the door opened so hard that it slammed back against the wall. Slocum had his six-gun halfway drawn before he saw the tall, gaunt man with a medical bag outlined against the sun.

"You shoulda called me sooner. This gent's about ready to be planted six feet under."

"You double as the town gravedigger?" Slocum asked. He didn't bother keeping the sarcasm from his voice.

"I don't have to tend him, you know." The doctor glared at Slocum. Bloodshot eyes attested to how much booze he had put away.

"Yes, you do." Slocum's voice was low and level. The doctor jumped as if Slocum had jammed a knife into his belly. The cold stare and the way Slocum's hand rested on the butt of his Colt dictated what the doctor had to do.

"My job," the doctor mumbled, kneeling beside the bench and opening his bag. "Don't have to get nasty about it. I know what I'm doin'."

Slocum backed away and collapsed in Rasumussen's desk chair. The manager started to complain, then saw the expression on Slocum's face. Without a word, he handed over the bottle and what little remained of its contents.

Twenty minutes later, the doctor stood, snapped his bag shut, and said, "He'll be all right. Don't give him no whiskey for a day or two. Nothing but water, no matter how loud he squeals. And give him a tablespoon of this every couple hours." He tossed a bottle of yellowish liquid to Rasumussen and then glared at Slocum. Without another word, the doctor left.

"Is that stuff going to kill Smitty or cure him?" Slocum asked, pointing at the bottle.

"Damned if I know. The first dose might not make a difference. If he survives the second, that must mean he'll pull through. He can sleep here, but I need to rustle up a couple blankets. Hold the fort, Slocum, while I find some horse blankets."

Rasumussen had barely left out the back to go to the storage shed when a blue-uniformed young lieutenant and a much older sergeant entered. Slocum considered finishing off Smitty's medicine to soothe his own growing thirst. His mouth felt like the inside of a cotton bale and he needed twenty-four solid hours of sleep. He felt he had worn out his welcome in Eagle Pass and found nothing more to keep him here.

His reverie about his time with Consuela, as he wondered where she might be now, was brought up short by the lieutenant slapping his canvas gloves held in his left hand against the palm of his right hand. The noise cracked like a blacksnake whip in the small depot office.

"You the man who found the cut in the telegraph line?"

"Reckon I am," Slocum said.

"You've done a great service to everyone in Eagle Pass. Loss of communication means possible danger for them."

"Like the Apaches attacking the way station on the road north to Fort Davis?" Slocum saw that the lieutenant hadn't known anything about the attack.

"They're going after water," Slocum went on. "The best that Smitty over there and Jesse, the way station agent, could figure, you've cut them off from their usual watering holes. That makes attacking the spots where there is water all the more important to them."

"How many?" asked the lieutenant.

"Can't rightly say, but it was close to a couple dozen. We done what we could to kill as many as possible. That was probably five or six. Then we ran off the rest."

"How many were you?"

"Six men from some Indian commission, Jesse, Smitty, and me."

The lieutenant snorted in disgust.

"I thought you were giving a valid report, not spinning a tall tale. Nine men driving off more than twenty Apache braves?" The lieutenant shook his head.

"Believe what you will, Lieutenant," Slocum said, "but that's what happened. If you get on out to the way station, you might track down some of them. Or they might have returned, scalped Jesse, and stolen away as much Butterfield water as they can drink."

Jonah Rasumussen returned, blankets piled in his arms. He dropped them on the floor.

"I see you gents got together whilst I was out. Did Slocum tell you what happened?"

"If this man is Slocum, he gave me a highly improbable tale that cast himself in the best possible light."

"That's Slocum and he probably did nothing of the sort. Did he tell you he stampeded what horses were in the corral—after stealing them back from the Apaches—and made them think an entire company of cavalry was onto them?"

"Is it the heat, Mr. Rasumussen? You're all going plumb crazy from the heat?"

"I'd advise you to see what Jesse has to say. He's out there all by his lonesome," Rasumussen said.

"We've found signs that a band of hostiles is in the area," the lieutenant said. "It's best if I go find them." He spun and marched out as if he were on a parade ground.

The sergeant lingered. He squinted at Slocum, then scratched himself and finally said, "I seen you before. You're the gent what saved the settlers after they tried to get across the Pecos a couple months back."

"Did that," Slocum allowed. "It was last year sometime."

"Thank you," the sergeant said. "That was my sister and brother-in-law in that broke-down Conestoga. Old Rafe's not got the sense God gave a goose, and my sister's not much better for marryin' him, but they ain't liars. They said you were real heroic rescuin' them. Caught sight of you as you rode out of town then."

Slocum had nothing to say. He remembered the incident. He had done what any man would seeing a woman struggling to get a wagon across a raging river. It was only after he had rescued her and the wagon that he had learned her husband had been hit on the head and washed out of the wagon. Finding him hadn't been too hard. The man had washed up less than a quarter mile downstream and some miracle had kept him alive.

"More 'n twenty Injuns?" The sergeant looked hard at him.

"Not anymore. As I told the lieutenant, we killed a few."

"You killed more 'n a few's my guess," the sergeant said. "Much obliged. I'll see that the shavetail don't get into too much trouble, this bein' his first field engagement and all."

"Water," Slocum said. "Find the watering holes and you'll have them."

The sergeant ran out when the officer bellowed at him.

Slocum leaned back and closed his eyes. Weariness washed over him like a tidal wave. He thought on Consuela and Smitty and the Butterfield line and how he wanted to be on his way.

"They haven't found him yet," Rasumussen said.

"Who's that?" Slocum opened his eyes. The room hadn't changed.

"El Loco. They've been huntin' for him since you rolled out of the depot. He's a wily one, what for havin' a screw loose in his head and all," Rasumussen said.

"He didn't shoot anybody in the back. He might be El Loco, but he's not a murderer, not like that."

"No sign of the wagon we lost either. The telegraph being down put a real crimp in finding what's happened to it. Lost at least two men on it, along with the cargo."

"What was it carrying?" Slocum asked. He didn't care, but this seemed like a reasonable enough question.

"You've 'bout earned that horse," Rasumussen said unexpectedly. "You still have a few days to go till the month's up, but the way you delivered the passengers while fighting off Apaches makes it seem like I owe you."

To ride on out of Eagle Pass. The idea struck Slocum as a good one. Crazy Mexicans and naive lieutenants and deadly Apaches made the area one he would prefer to look back on rather than dealing with it on a daily basis.

"You can take the mare. The one with the white blaze. I used to ride her on occasion, but decided I liked the gelding better," Rasumussen said.

"Thanks. I'll stick around long enough to see how Smitty gets on," Slocum said. He appreciated it that Rasumussen understood what was going on without the need to ask.

"You got a week's pay coming, too. There ought to be a reward after you saved Jesse and the way station."

"You're taking my word for it all?"

"I'm not like that damned snot-nosed lieutenant. He couldn't find an Apache if he was being scalped," Rasumussen said. "Still, it's better to have him and his company out prowlin' about than to have them stay down south where it's safe. The troop at Fort Davis can use all the help they can get."

"Heard that the fort's colonel, Grierson by name, keeps his soldiers out in the field all the time."

"He's about the only commander General Sherman could find that'd put up with a fort full of coloreds."

"I'll get me a drink over at the Hijinx and be back to see after Smitty."

The driver moaned softly and thrashed about weakly at the mention of his name, showing he was still among the living. Slocum counted that feverish groan as a good sign. Smitty had rallied whenever necessary while they'd been on the road. He was a fighter and only needed a few days to heal. He might even survive the yellow piss-colored medicine the doctor had left for him.

Slocum couldn't tell if he preferred the sun beating down on him and sucking every drop of water from his body or the cold air that descended over the desert at night. Then he figured it didn't matter as long as he had something to complain about. Enough of the citizens in Eagle Pass and the surrounding miles of desert were six feet under and not complaining about a damned thing any longer.

He had started into the saloon when movement out of the corner of his eye caused him to sink down into a crouch. His hand rested on the ebony butt of his six-shooter. He let the pistol drop back when he saw Consuela motioning to him. A fleeting memory of the first time they had met crossed his mind. The situation had been identical, her calling to him from that very alley. That might have been a hundred years ago for all that had happened since.

Slocum went to her and started to kiss her, but she pulled away.

"Oh, John, you have to help him. I know you tried before."

"Rodrigo? I figured he would be back across the Rio Grande where he belonged after the cowboy got shot."

"He killed no one! He was framed!"

"Who'd do a thing like that?"

"You know who. Duke Denham," she said, spitting the name out as if it burned her tongue.

"I'm not saying you're wrong, but if you hie on across the river and go home, Denham won't be able to do anything to you."

"It is not me he wants. He will use me to get to his end, but he cares nothing for me!"

"Then he's a damned fool," Slocum said.

Consuela lost a touch of her anger, then smiled weakly.

"You are a kind man, John Slocum. No matter what you do, you are a kind man. But no. Denham wants Rodrigo and will use me to lure him."

"All the more reason to go home," Slocum said.

"Find him for me. My brother is not right in the head, but he is no killer. Denham framed him so the law would help find Rodrigo."

"Heard tell there was a reward on his head."

"Denham put it up. He wants my brother alive. There is no reward if he is dead."

"Why not? If Denham's out to get your brother, what's he care if he's dead?"

"For me, John, do this thing. Find Rodrigo and get him away from them. Do not let Denham or Marshal Atkinson capture him."

"You make it sound as if they already had caught him. Do you know where he is?" Slocum felt the weight of the world crushing down on his shoulders. It wasn't enough that he had rescued Don Rodrigo once before. Now he had to do it a second time, and this time there was a good chance he was helping a murderer who shot an unarmed man in the back.

"I don't know where he is, but you are a clever tracker. You find him. For me, John, for me." Consuela looked apprehensive, then stood on tiptoe and started to kiss him. He held her at arm's length.

"If I get him across the river into Mexico, will you promise to keep him there?"

"Oh, yes, John, *sí*!"

He wanted to kiss her, but one thing would lead to another and there was no time. The way she felt like wood in his arms told him she would do anything to get him to help her brother. That wasn't the way Slocum wanted it.

"The best source of information I've got is inside the barroom," he told her. Consuela bit her lower lip and nodded.

"You will find him for me. I know you will." She turned and vanished around the corner of the building without even a backward glance. Something had changed Consuela, and Slocum reckoned it was Duke Denham and what he had done to her. Slocum considered getting that horse Rasumussen had promised him and simply leaving Eagle Pass. He could be ten miles down the road before darkness forced him to stop.

Then he thought better of it. Finding El Loco was the best way of getting to Duke Denham and putting a bullet in his black heart. For what he had done to Consuela, Denham deserved to die. More than this, Slocum would enjoy killing the man for the hell of it.

He went into the Hijinx and got a bottle. Sitting with his back to a wall, he watched the cowboys slowly coming into the saloon after a hard day's work. They would be liquored up and piled into wagons before midnight for their bosses to drive home. He listened to their chatter, but heard nothing to help find Don Rodrigo. He slowly drank down the contents of the whiskey and felt his own aches go away. But the problems remained.

Slocum looked up when he heard a commotion outside. Luther swung open the doors and went directly to the bar, followed by a dozen men. Slocum recognized a few as townspeople, but all pressed close to the outlaw. Luther didn't see Slocum, and that was fine because the name El Loco rose above the din.

"We got to find that maverick and bring him in for the marshal," Luther said loudly. "There's a reward out on El Loco's head, but I say it's not enough."

"It's danged near twenty dollars," somebody said.

"I'll add thirty. That's *fifty* dollars reward total and complete for El Loco, but only if you bring him in alive and kickin'. We ain't savages. We don't take the law into our own hands. We let a judge and jury string 'im up for killing poor ole Bob Ed."

A cheer went up. It didn't take much imagination for Slocum to decide that Bob Ed was the cowboy who had been gunned down. The sound of Luther's voice told plenty about the outlaw's involvement in that killing, but no one in the crowd heard it. The majestic sum of fifty dollars lured them on, and no one asked the obvious question. Why would Luther spend a dime of his own money to see an outlaw brought to justice?

"We need to send out scouts," Luther went on. "Maybe a dozen or so. I'll pay a dollar a day to any man willin' to hunt fer El Loco."

This caused Slocum to sit up in his chair. Luther was offering a lot of money out of his own pocket to find Don Rodrigo. What was Duke Denham's interest in the Mexican? Did he think that threatening Rodrigo would make Consuela do whatever he pleased? Slocum doubted that, but he had no better answer.

He hunkered down in his chair again to keep from being seen as Luther led the crowd outside and down the street toward another saloon. It was obvious the outlaw wanted the word to spread that a big reward had been laid on El Loco's head.

Alive.

9

Slocum watched half a dozen men ride out, each with a couple bright, new silver dollars jangling in their pockets. Luther looked smug as his paid scouts left Eagle Pass, but Slocum was more interested in seeing what Denham's henchman did when the scouts returned. Until then, he could content himself with trailing the outlaw. He followed Luther down the street and suddenly lost him. Wary now, Slocum backtracked, squeezed between two buildings leaning together and supporting each other, then popped out behind them. Ten yards away Luther stood with his six-shooter drawn, waiting to plug anyone on his tail.

Pressing back into the tight space between the buildings, Slocum peered around now and then to be sure Luther remained where he was. If he came in this direction, he would spot Slocum in an instant. After a respectable time, Slocum chanced another quick look. Luther had holstered his six-gun and shuffled about, kicking at rocks and looking out to the east. He took fixings from his pocket and rolled a smoke, lit the cigarette, finished it in quick, hard puffs, and began pacing. Slocum had seen men waiting impatiently before, but this was a textbook example. The eventual sound of hoof-beats told Slocum that Luther's wait was about over.

Looking around the corner of the building again, Slocum reached for his Colt, but checked his draw when he identified the rider. Duke Denham stepped down from his horse and pressed close to his partner. Slocum heard Luther plainly, but Denham only croaked. A smile came to Slocum's lips when he saw the way the outlaw leader had his bandanna wrapped tightly around his neck as if it held a poultice. In their brief fight, Slocum had done more than just laying out the outlaw. Denham wouldn't be barking orders again because of a damaged voice box. His words came out in a painful whisper Slocum could hardly hear.

"We got to find him soon, boss," Luther said.

"Send 'em all out?" croaked Denham.

"Yup, got half a dozen of them drunks from the saloon out scoutin' for that son of a bitch. He can't keep hidin' from us forever. It's like usin' a shotgun. Don't have to do much aimin'. Send enough men out and one of 'em's sure to spot him."

"Soon, we gotta get him soon 'n pry the facts from him. Others huntin' fer it."

Slocum frowned. What were they talking about? The way Duke Denham talked—barely whispered—they wanted Don Rodrigo because of something he knew. It came as a relief they weren't intent on using Rodrigo as a hostage to force Consuela to be Denham's sex slave, but it raised more questions that only El Loco could answer. What had he gotten himself into that involved Denham and his gang?

"How 'bout Slocum?" Denham tensed as he asked the question, and his hand went to the butt of his six-shooter. It was as if he visualized his enemy standing in front of him and was going to take care of business then and there.

Slocum slid back a little, worried Denham might have spotted him.

"Far as I can tell, he got a horse from the Butterfield man and is fixin' on hightailin' it outta town. He's a drifter and won't stick around much longer."

"I want him dead. He kept us from robbin' the stage twice." Duke Denham reached up and put his hand on his bandaged throat. Just the light touch made him wince. Slocum wanted to walk over to the man and finish the job. Another punch wouldn't be as satisfying as clamping his hands around the neck and squeezing until Denham breathed his last.

"Let it go, Duke. We got bigger fish to fry," Luther said. The man staggered back when Denham shoved him hard.

"I owe Slocum. When we find El Loco and get what we need from him, I'm settlin' the score. The doc says I'll talk like this the rest of my born days."

Slocum almost stepped out, drew, and fired a killing shot to make that prediction come true then and there. He would have if two more men hadn't popped out of the alley behind Luther. He didn't recognize them but from the way they were greeted, they were in Denham's gang.

They held a low-voiced confab that Slocum couldn't even catch the drift of. Whatever they said, it agitated Denham and left Luther looking sullen. The outlaw leader swung into the saddle and rode off at a gallop. Luther and the other two quickly left, going back down the alley toward Eagle Pass's main street.

Slocum leaned against the building, staring at the spot where Denham and Luther had made their mysterious plans for Don Rodrigo. It didn't make a whole lot of sense that the Mexican knew anything that would be of value to the outlaws, but it seemed that way to Denham. Slocum could not dispute how Denham wanted to fill him full of holes either. If the shoe had been on the other foot, Slocum would have wanted revenge on Denham for making him sound like a frog. The time would come when Denham's croaking stopped entirely because Slocum wasn't going to lose that contest.

But, like Denham, Slocum realized finding Don Rodrigo mattered most.

* * *

"Is there anywhere he felt comfortable? A place he trusted everyone around him?" Slocum asked Consuela. "He might be crazy as a loon, but he has to nest somewhere." He looked around the small room Consuela had taken during her stay in Eagle Pass. The furnishings were spartan and consisted of little more than a corn-husk mattress thrown on the floor and a low stool holding a porcelain washbasin. Where the pitcher had gotten off to, he had no idea. Maybe a pitcher cost more and Consuela could not afford it. This boardinghouse did not cater to those able to pay for such luxuries. There wasn't even a thunder mug in sight, and the outhouse was a long walk outside and down into a ravine.

"He is unpredictable," Consuela said. The worry in her voice was mirrored on her lovely face. "He sometimes talked of Chupadero Springs."

"That's thirty, forty miles south of here, along the river," Slocum said.

"There is a cantina. The bartender does not throw him out whenever he goes in. I think the man laughs at Rodrigo and makes him say and do things for the amusement of the other patrons."

"That's likely," Slocum said. He had seen saloons where they catered to village idiots for the same reason. Entertainment was hard to come by on the frontier. "At least he's getting free whiskey."

Consuela glared at him.

"I mean that he's not got more men hunting for him to pay old bills," Slocum said. He realized how lame that sounded and how it irritated Consuela even more. "What's the name of the place?"

She shrugged her fine shoulders. "I do not know, and he might not be there. It is a long way to ride on a wild-goose chase."

"You're more likely to know where he's come to roost than them," Slocum said, jerking his thumb over his shoulder in the direction of the Hijinx. "What's Denham want with him anyway? It's got to do with something other than using him as a bargaining chip to get you into his bed."

"Oh, Duke Denham is likely to try anything. He is a terrible man."

"No argument on that score, but I overheard him talking with Luther. They want your brother for reasons that don't have to do with you."

"Not with me? That sounds so . . . wrong. What man wouldn't want me?" Consuela moved closer and pressed warmly into him. She rubbed up and down slowly, drawing her breasts across his arm. Slocum began to respond to her nearness. Her scent, her warmth, the feel of her firm young body, and the way she boldly shoved her hand down across his belly made him harder by the second.

"Is this what you want to do?" he asked.

"Isn't it what *you* want to do?" She moved around and pressed her chest against his. Her head tipped back slightly. Eyes half closed and lips parted, she made for a temptation Slocum was not strong enough to avoid. He kissed her. The soft lips tasted sweeter than honey, and the way her arms circled his body and pulled him closer left no doubt what she wanted.

The same as him.

They turned slowly, locked in each other's arms, as they kissed. The spiral took them to their knees on the mattress. Slocum ignored the tiny cloud of dust rising as they dropped full length. He was too engrossed in the woman and her charms to be fussy about anything else under him. Side by side, they explored each other. Slocum ran his fingers down her side, across her clothed thigh, and then began bunching up her skirt to expose a perfect brown leg.

His hand slipped farther up under the skirt and felt the warm, willing flesh. Consuela moaned softly as he worked upward over her bare thigh and then between her legs. The dampness welling there told him how ready for him she was. He moved up a bit more so his hand cupped her mound. He pressed down a little and brought a cry of pleasure to her lips.

"Oh, John, this is what I want. Strip me naked and make love to me." She worked to open her plain peasant blouse and exposed her naked breasts to him. Rays of sunlight slanted between boards in the wall and highlighted those cones as surely as any stage spotlight could. He eased off her blouse and got her bare to the waist, but his eyes drank in the glory of those breasts. Brown, firm, capped with ruddy nipples.

He took first one and then the other into his mouth, using tongue and teeth while he sucked. She thrashed about under him and lifted her hips off the mattress. As she did so, he worked her skirt away. Her legs scissored back and forth in her hurry to get free of the skirt. Slocum never abandoned her breasts, moving back and forth from one to the other, but now he had to use both hands to pull her unwanted skirt away.

When she sank back to the mattress, she had achieved her goal of getting naked for him. But Slocum felt more discomfort than pleasure because of the way he was trapped in his jeans.

"Let me," Consuela said. She gently pushed him back so he could come up to his knees. Her nimble fingers stripped him of his coat, vest, and shirt while he discarded his gun belt.

Then she worked at his jeans and got them unbuttoned. He let out a gasp of relief as his erection sprang free. The sight of her bare and eager made him even more eager to put his tool to use.

She took the tip in her mouth and sucked hard. Slocum sagged down to the mattress. He kicked off his boots while she worked to get his jeans off. Her mouth never left him. Soft lips and agile tongue worked over his most sensitive flesh and caused him to quiver. He fought to keep from being like a young buck out for the first time, but it became harder when Consuela devoted her full attention to him. Her fingers stroked his balls as her mouth worked on his hardened length.

He ran his fingers through her jet-black hair and guided her in a rhythm that sent tremors throughout his balls and belly. When he was sure he couldn't take an instant more, he pushed her away.

"Now," he said. He pressed his hands into her breasts and moved her about so she was flat on her back. Her legs parted wantonly for him. He poised between her uplifted legs and looked down at her beautiful face. Even if he had wanted to now, there was no holding back. He fell forward and caught himself on his hands as his hips thrust forward. They both cried out when the blunt tip of his manhood brushed across her nether lips. Consuela wiggled her hips and positioned herself better. Slocum took advantage of this as he levered himself forward and sank deeply into her heated core.

She brought her knees up until she was doubled over. She let out tiny sounds of stark desire that spurred Slocum on. He began a slow pistoning motion, but quickly realized this was not going to work. He sped up. Friction mounted along his length and spread through her like wildfire. Consuela gasped, moaned, and began thrashing about. Her fingers clawed at his upper arms and back as she sat up halfway on the mattress.

When she sank back, he drove ever deeper, and then the world exploded all around them both. Slocum finished and dropped atop her, his weight pressing down into her. Consuela wrapped her arms around him and held him in place when he tried to roll to the side.

"I like the feel of your body on top of me," she whispered hotly in his ear. For some time they lay that way. Slocum wasn't sure who shifted or if it mattered.

They ended up side by side in each other's arms. Consuela pressed her cheek against his chest so he could feel her soft, warm breath rustle through his chest hair.

"You are so much a man in all ways," she said. "You will find my brother. I know you will return him safely to me."

Slocum guessed what his reward would be when he did. And it wasn't likely to be any paltry fifty dollars either.

10

"There's no need for you to come," Slocum said, exasperated. He faced Consuela and saw the set to her jaw. She was determined to accompany him on the hunt for her brother.

"He will not listen to you if you find him in Chupadero Springs," Consuela said. "I can talk to him. But I cannot find him by myself. Therefore, if he is to live, we must work together. You find him, I will talk him into going back to Mexico."

"Seems we did that once and it didn't work," Slocum said. "Any reason why he came back?" He saw the sudden slyness in her face. It passed in an instant, but there was a reason Don Rodrigo had returned to the U.S. side of the Rio Grande, and it had nothing to do with him being crazy.

"We must find him and ask," she said. "We cannot ask if we cannot find him."

"So we both ride for Chupadero Springs to find him," Slocum said, giving in. "It'll be dangerous on the trail. You know how the Apaches are raiding all the way to San Antonio now. I heard rumors that Nana and Victorio's sister, Lozen, are kicking the hell out of settlements all over South Texas."

"And Duke Denham is still in Eagle Pass," she said. "With such danger all about, is it not safer for me to ride with a man who can defend me?" She moved closer and put her hand on his stubbled cheek. "A man who can use his gun so well?" That hand slid down his chest and across his belt buckle. He caught her wrist before she could drift even lower. He wanted to be on the trail now, and if she kept this up there would have to be a delay.

"It might not be safer with me than remaining in your room."

"Room, pah," she said. Her lip curled and she waved her hand in a dismissive gesture. "That hovel is too poor to even be called a room."

"Seems to me you didn't have any complaints about the mattress last night."

Consuela smiled. It was as if the sun had risen for a second time that day.

"Some hardships are best shared together." Her hand slipped free of his grip, and she grabbed for his crotch. "Just as some hardness is best shared."

"Saddle up. We're already looking at a hot, dry ride."

Consuela stood on tiptoe and gave him a quick kiss before rushing off to get her horse. Slocum made sure he had a spare canteen filled to overflowing from a water barrel since he wasn't sure how well she would fare under the burning West Texas sun. While he waited for her, he looked around Eagle Pass. It wasn't such a bad place, he decided, if you ignored the old coot they had for a marshal who caved under pressure, or the Butterfield stagecoach agent who was sure every trip out would get robbed—and most were. Slocum considered going to pay his respects to Smitty but as the idea came to him, Consuela rode up. He was pleased to see she had two canteens of her own.

"You look surprised," she said, putting a hand on one canteen. "I have lived in the Chihuahua Desert all my life. Once away from the Rio Grande, water is scarce."

"Let's go. We might not reach Chupadero Springs today, but I want to get close."

"We could spend the night on the trail," Consuela said, looking dreamy. "It gets very cold in the desert. We would have to furnish each other warmth."

"This isn't a pleasure jaunt," Slocum said. "The sooner we corral your brother, the sooner he'll be safe."

"You can come with us to the hacienda in Mexico. We can spend much time together there."

"Yeah, the hacienda," Slocum said, wondering if Consuela was getting as crazy as her brother. He doubted she lived in much better quarters in Mexico than she had in Eagle Pass. The only difference was one of familiarity.

He put his heels to the mare's flanks and brought the horse to a fast walk. Consuela rode hard to catch up. By the time they had left the last of Eagle Pass far behind, he slowed and asked, "Do you know the road to Chupadero Springs?"

"It is ahead a few miles. There is a fork. The Butterfield stage route goes southeast toward San Antonio, and the smaller road angles toward the river and follows it into Chupadero Springs."

He nodded and set off again, keeping the pace fast. When their horses began to tire, he slowed, then brought them up to a trot and back to a walk. Varying the gait kept them moving through the crushing heat and devoured the distance without killing the horses.

They spoke little as they traveled. For that Slocum was glad. His mouth had turned to a gummy swamp barely out of town. Whatever moisture was there disappeared quickly, forcing him to use an old Apache trick of rolling a small stone around to build the spit. Even then he found himself longing to take a deep drink from a canteen—deep enough to drain it.

He drifted, swathed in heat and bathed in sunlight. His thoughts roamed all over, from Don Rodrigo to Consuela and Duke Denham to things he had done and seen months and years before. When he could no longer keep memory separate from the road ahead, he would take a small sip of water. Even so, he had drained both canteens by the time they reached Chupadero Springs.

The sun had set, turning the air cold within minutes. Rocks and baked earth lost heat rapidly, and a brisk wind blew off the nearby river, making it seem even colder. The town had formed a mile from the Rio Grande, centered around a plaza with a well. Whether the water came from the Rio Grande or bubbled up like it did around Limpio Creek near Fort Davis, he neither knew nor cared. It meant he didn't have to ride any longer.

He groaned as he stepped down from his horse and felt the weight on his legs again. His mare tossed her head and seemed downright frisky at the lack of weight on her.

"Where's the cantina?"

Consuela remained on her horse. She stared into the dark town as if she had never seen it before.

"I do not know, but Rodrigo has mentioned it. How difficult can it be to find?"

"You've got a point." Slocum led his mare to the well and pulled up a couple buckets of water. It felt good on his face as he splashed it into a shallow watering trough. When their horses had drunk their fill, Slocum said, "Stay here. I'll go find the cantina."

"Alone?"

"You've got the horses," Slocum said. "And you also have a derringer tucked away, unless I miss my guess." He laughed as Consuela's hand went to her broad cloth sash. As the day wore on and the woman sweat in the desert heat, the outline of the tiny weapon had become increasingly clear. If she wanted to use the derringer, she would have to peel the sweat-soaked cloth off it first.

"You have been watching me," she accused.

"All day, all the time," Slocum said. He laughed at her expression. "You're a sight prettier than the desert. It never changes."

Consuela sputtered as Slocum went toward a sudden

burst of boisterous laughter. If anyplace in Chupadero Springs would cause such mirth, it would be the cantina. He twisted through the winding streets and saw a small thatched awning over a door on an adobe building. From inside came the laughter and loud voices. Slocum made certain his six-shooter was resting easy in its cross-draw holster and then went inside.

The instant he stepped through the door, the laughter stopped and all eyes turned to him. He ignored the silence and went to the bar.

"Tequila," he said, preferring it to the rotgut trade whiskey he was likely to get otherwise.

The barkeep put a shot glass in front of him and said, "Five."

Slocum dropped a dime on the bar, but the barkeep shook his head sadly.

"Five *dollars*."

"That's a mighty steep price to pay for a shot of lousy tequila," Slocum said. He downed the liquor and sucked in his breath at its powerful kick. "Don't reckon you sell much at that price." He dropped a five-dollar greenback on the bar, but pinned the barkeep's hand down with his own when the man reached for it.

"You are hurting me."

"If I pay that much for a shot of tequila, I want something with it." The man tried to jerk free, but Slocum had the leverage and held him firmly. "Do you know a man named Don Rodrigo de la Madrid y Garza?"

"No, no one of that name."

Slocum leaned forward and applied more pressure, causing the barkeep to sink to his knees behind the bar or have his wrist broken.

"Might be you know him by the name El Loco."

"You want him?"

"Where can I find him?"

"You are a gunfighter? You will kill the *pendejo*?"

Slocum waited. The barkeep's answer came rushing out in a torrent of Spanish and English. Slocum followed enough in each language to get the gist.

"So El Loco's going around pretending to be a gunman?"

"Yes!"

Slocum released the barkeep's wrist. The man rubbed it and looked fiercely at him. Slocum vowed not to turn his back on the man.

"Where is he? I'll take care of him for you." Slocum looked around the room and saw a mixture of hatred and anticipation on the faces. Not much happened in a sleepy border town like Chupadero Springs, but when it did, it usually proved both violent and bloody.

"This time of day he walks the main street shooting at people. Then he comes here."

Slocum left the cantina. Finding the town's main street couldn't be any harder than locating the cantina. He returned to the well where Consuela waited anxiously. She jumped to her feet and rushed to him.

"You have found him?"

"This look like the town's main street?" Slocum asked, pointing into the dusk down one street wider than the others leading to the plaza with its well.

"I suppose. Why?"

"Rodrigo has taken it into his head that he is a gunfighter and is causing all kinds of hell. I'm surprised someone hasn't taken him up on a fight."

"John, be careful. My brother is most adept with a sixgun. He is not a gunfighter, but he is good enough."

"Good enough to scare off the local young bucks wanting a quick reputation?" This surprised him. Don Rodrigo had not seemed all that violent, in spite of his protestations to the contrary.

"Do not harm him. Please. He is my brother." She clung to Slocum and then released him. "Find him. Quickly."

Slocum headed down the wider street, keeping a sharp eye out for movement in the gathering shadows. He didn't want a bullet in the back, though he doubted Don Rodrigo would try to kill him that way. He was off in the head, but not all that wild. If he fancied himself a gunman, he would want to face down his opponent. Slocum hoped it didn't come to that since only one of them was likely to walk away. Telling Consuela he had killed her brother wasn't something Slocum cottoned to much.

His hand instinctively went for his Colt when the shot rang out. He came out of his crouch, but kept his six-shooter in hand as he advanced. He had seen the muzzle flash from the pistol as it fired, and now went directly toward the spot where the shot had been fired.

"Don Rodrigo? That you?"

"It is I, El Terrible! I am the scourge of the entire Rio Grande! From one end to the other!" Rodrigo fired two more shots into the air. Slocum heard shutters slamming and feet pounding on the ground as the residents fled.

"I've got somebody you'd like to meet."

"Who are you? Ah, you are Slocum. I remember you. The lawman from Eagle Pass."

"I was shotgun guard on the stage you tried to hold up. I escorted you across the Rio Grande so you could go home with Consuela."

"Where is my lovely sister? She should revel in the fear I, El Terrible, cause in their hearts!" He fired twice more. One bullet tore away a corner of a mud brick house.

Slocum wondered if Don Rodrigo had one more round in the six-shooter or if he had expended it earlier. There was no way to tell that didn't run the risk of getting that slug in his belly.

"I have heard you are the finest marksman in all of Mexico," Slocum said. "Can you hit that crow? The one on the roof?" He pointed out the bird some distance away perched on a viga sticking out from the adobe building.

Slocum blinked when Rodrigo spun and fired. The air filled with feathers as the bird fell to the ground. Don Rodrigo was either the luckiest man in the world or a crack shot.

"Can you do better?" Don Rodrigo asked.

Slocum moved like a striking snake. He closed the distance between them and, as Don Rodrigo turned, grabbed the six-gun and twisted hard. The barrel was warm, but not hot enough to burn his hand as he forced it up and yanked it out of the man's hand.

"Come on," Slocum said. He thrust Don Rodrigo's pistol into his belt and grabbed the man by the collar. Cloth tore. He got a better grip and hauled him along the street.

"You cannot do this. I challenge you to a fight!"

"Your sister will explain it all," Slocum said.

"Consuela is here? She comes to watch me kill you!"

Slocum's patience was wearing thin. He manhandled the struggling would-be gunman back to the plaza and considered tossing Don Rodrigo into the well to cool him off a mite. He never got the chance. Consuela rushed forward and embraced her brother. They chattered in Spanish while Slocum looked around, wondering if anyone would complain if he took a horse for Rodrigo. It seemed a fair exchange, one horse for getting rid of a dangerous annoyance.

"Where's your horse?" Slocum asked. Don Rodrigo pointed, and Slocum saw a horse tethered not far off that looked like the one he had last seen Rodrigo astride. Closer examination showed a worn Mexican saddle that, in its day, had been expensive. While there might be any number of such rigs in a border town, Slocum took it as a sign this was Don Rodrigo's horse. No one peering out from behind partially opened doors protested as he led it back to the well.

"We are to ride together," Don Rodrigo said proudly. "You will be my sidekick, no?"

"No," Slocum said, silencing Consuela with a glare. "We're riding out of town. Now."

"To the countryside. We will be the scourge of the lawless!" Don Rodrigo put his heels to his horse's flanks and rocketed away. Slocum climbed into the saddle and trotted along beside Consuela.

"He is looking for outlaws now," she said in a weak voice. "That is good. He will not gun down innocent people if he thinks he is a lawman."

"His six-shooter's empty," Slocum said, drawing it from his belt. "I don't think it's safe to give this back to him."

"He doesn't miss it," she said, looking out into the darkness.

Slocum brought his horse to a trot. It was going to be a real chore keeping up with El Loco's wild mood swings. One minute he was a desperado, and the next a marshal upholding the law. Getting Don Rodrigo out of his hair was something Slocum looked forward to, as much as he would be loath to bid Consuela adios.

"There he is, down in the arroyo," Consuela called.

Slocum rode over and saw that Rodrigo had jumped off his horse and looked around as if he were a conquistador claiming the New World for Spain.

"This is where we will spend the night. A noble *tierra*."

Slocum got his mare down the steep, crumbling embankment and rode about to better see the spot the vaquero had chosen for their camp. Camping in a dry riverbed was foolish most times, but it was late summer and there wouldn't be any unexpected runoff from the distant mountains. If a flash flood washed through, Slocum reckoned he could drink his fill before drowning. He had forgotten to refill his canteens from the Chupadero Springs well.

"Here. I will sleep here. You will be there, dear sister. And my amigo will stand guard."

"You don't have to do as he says, John," Consuela said softly. "There is no danger here."

"Nope." Slocum wished he and Consuela could share a bedroll, but that wasn't going to happen with Don Rodrigo making such a pest of himself. The man fluttered about like a butterfly with a broken wing, giving orders, doing chores for himself, and finally sinking down under his blanket beside a small fire after an unsatisfactory dinner of jerky and what little water remained in their canteens.

"I am sorry, John," Consuela said. "I did not think to refill the canteens."

"I'm not going back into Chupadero Springs for water," Slocum said. "We might find a spring nearby. If we spot an army patrol, we can ask. Otherwise, it's only an hour's ride to the Rio Grande. We can drink our fill then."

"Before we go into Mexico," Consuela said sadly. She brightened and said, "You can come with us, John. I would like that."

"I would, too," Slocum said, "but it's best if you and Rodrigo go ahead on your own. If I rode with you, it'd only upset him more."

Don Rodrigo de la Madrid y Garza snored loudly on the far side of the fire.

"You are right," Consuela said, once more morose. She smiled weakly and said, "You are a good man, John Slocum."

Slocum wondered if she realized that he had sought a way to separate himself from her and her troublesome brother and the small lie he had just told was it. For all the nights of pleasure he might spend with Consuela, the days would be filled with her crazy brother's antics. That sort of vexation Slocum wanted to avoid.

He pulled his blanket around him, scooted around to dig depressions for his hips and shoulders in the sandy arroyo bottom, and went to sleep. He came awake just before dawn, hand reaching for his six-shooter.

Slocum took a few seconds to get the sleep cobwebs remaining in his head cleared away, then slowly rolled over, Colt Navy ready for action. Something had awakened him, but he could not tell at first what it was, and then it came in a rush.

He was alone. Don Rodrigo and Consuela, along with their horses, were gone.

11

Slocum circled the campsite and saw nothing to show a fight had occurred. Lacking any evidence that Don Rodrigo and his sister had been abducted, Slocum had to consider himself lucky that he was free of them. Still, it stuck in his craw that Consuela had left without so much as a handshake after all he had done for her and her brother.

He ate a solitary breakfast, choking it down with the last of his water. Before he hit the trail, he had to find more or he would be mighty thirsty come noontime. As he rolled up his blanket and prepared to saddle his mare, he heard a distant sound. At first he couldn't identify it. In a few minutes, it came loud and clear through the still morning air. Slocum drew his rifle from the saddle sheath and jacked in a round. He looked around for a good place to make a stand, and saw small boulders on the far side of the ravine.

"Come on," he said, tugging on his horse's bridle. "We've got some work to do before getting on the trail, and it's not likely to be pretty." The rocks were enough to shield him if he flopped on his belly, but he was worried that the horse would be exposed to gunfire.

That meant he had to make every shot count and drive off whoever came his way. The sounds he had heard convinced him this was not a cavalry company out on patrol. The miscellaneous sounds were more like a dozen undisciplined men, joshing one another and making loud boasts. That ruled out being approached by an Apache band. If anything, they were even more disciplined on the trail than the cavalry. All that remained was a gang of road agents.

Robbing a stagecoach or a pilgrim along the road amounted to the same thing for outlaws. Easy pickings. A few rounds pumped into his body left him for dead. Then they were free to steal his boots and saddle, horse, and any other belongings he might have. They'd be in luck, too, since Slocum still had a few dollars of his pay from the Butterfield job stuffed in his shirt pocket. His best chance lay in them missing him entirely.

He caught sight of a tall-crowned hat bobbing just above the far arroyo bank. Settling down, he drew a bead. Another hat came into view, then the upper torso of the rider. Slocum cursed his bad luck. For whatever reason, the one rider had decided to take a look into the deep arroyo.

Slocum's finger drew back slowly on the trigger. At this range he wasn't likely to miss.

"Hey, Bret, come take a look-see at this. Somebody camped down in the arroyo."

Slocum let his breath out slowly as he got the sight picture. He could drop the nosy rider and then get a good shot at his partner.

"Good eyeballin'," said the second rider. "Let's all git on down there and see how many spent the night."

Slocum had started to fire when the morning sun glinted off the man's chest. He squinted, moved the front sight on his rifle to the second rider, and then released the pressure on the trigger. He had been found by a posse led by a man wearing a badge. He didn't recognize either the first posse member or the lawman, but the only ones he really knew were Marshal Atkinson up in Eagle Pass and some of the posse he had whipped up to hunt for Don Rodrigo.

"Sheriff, there. Over there, behind them rocks!"

Slocum swung his rifle around to cover a third rider who had skidded down a steep bank ten yards away from the first two. On the rim of the arroyo behind were two more of the posse. If he fired one shot, he would have to fire a dozen. Slocum knew he wasn't in a defensible position to fight off this many men. His initial guess about the number in the posse proved accurate. He counted thirteen men poking their heads above the arroyo to see what was going on.

He almost laughed. If he had wanted, he could have taken out four or five of them. For a brief moment, he had wondered if these might be Texas Rangers, but no Ranger would ever silhouette himself foolishly against the sky, much less do so while staring into the rising sun.

He lowered his rifle and got to his feet. Talk was the only way he was going to walk away from this chance meeting.

"Who you, mister?" demanded the man wearing the badge. The sheriff had his six-shooter out and trained on Slocum.

Slocum set his rifle aside and kept his hands well away from his six-gun. Others in the posse were reaching for their six-shooters. If any of them got the least nervous, they would leave behind a corpse for the buzzards to fight over. Slocum wanted to avoid that at all costs since it would be his body weighed down by too much lead and the bulk of buzzards on his chest.

"I'm just traveling through on my way to Eagle Pass. I work for Jonah Rasumussen, the Butterfield manager. My name's Slocum."

He waited for some response. The sheriff didn't move to lower his six-gun.

"What you doin' down here?" the sheriff finally asked. "This is a ways from Eagle Pass."

"I had to hunt for downed telegraph wires. Rasumussen sent me on a chore for the company. You know Rasumussen, don't you?" Slocum lied to give himself some credibility. The Butterfield Stage agent was the only reputable businessman in the area that he knew who might be known also to a sheriff and a posse.

"I know Jonah," the sheriff said. "Your story's kinda weak, Mr. Slocum."

"You get in touch with Rasumussen. Ask if he knows me."

The sheriff hesitated a moment longer, then shoved his pistol into its holster.

"I fancy myself a judge of men tellin' the truth. Might be since I so seldom hear it from the varmints I catch. You sound like you know Jonah."

Slocum said nothing more. It never paid to sound too nervous or supply added details. A lawman waited for any small discrepancy, and would pounce on it like a coyote on a rabbit.

"You the one what camped here last night?"

Slocum said that he was, and added, "Who are you hunting for with so many men? The Duke Denham gang?"

"Don't know him. Mostly, I brought along more 'n I need for a posse 'cuz of the Apaches. I'm huntin' down a no-account what robbed a gold shipment."

"Could be Denham," Slocum said. "Marshal Atkinson in Eagle Pass has had trouble with him holding up the stage."

"Don't know him. This one, the one I'm huntin' for's named El Loco. Not real sure of his proper name. A Mexican who acts all loony."

"A gold shipment? There hasn't been one sent on the Butterfield line that didn't arrive since I took the job with Rasumussen." Even as he spoke, Slocum went cold inside. Rasumussen had mentioned a shipment being lost, but Slocum had not realized it had been gold.

"Been a week or so. We heard tell El Loco was spotted in Chupadero Springs shootin' up the place and actin' like he was cock of the walk. That brought me and the boys out."

"A big reward on him?"

"Butterfield is offerin' a tidy reward, but gettin' the gold back's enough for me. The shipment was carryin' close to twenty thousand dollars in coins. Damn fools thought they could sneak it through the desert with only one guard. Both the guard and driver was found. Least, I think it was them. The animals had a real banquet, but from the clothing that was left on their bones, I'm sure enough it was them."

Slocum tried not to show any surprise at the size of the missing shipment. It hardly seemed credible that Don Rodrigo was responsible, but the man had shown strange abilities. Slocum remembered the way he had accurately blasted the crow back in Chupadero Springs with a single shot. It might have been luck, but what if it wasn't? Maybe in his madness Rodrigo had robbed the gold shipment and killed two men. The cowboy in Eagle Pass had fallen to the vaquero's pistol as well.

He looked past the sheriff to the spot where he, Consuela, and Don Rodrigo had camped. Four of the posse walked their horses through the site, making it impossible for anyone to tell how many had actually camped there. For that incompetence, he heaved a sigh of relief.

"All I want to do is ride on, Sheriff," Slocum said.

"Ain't likely you're El Loco," the sheriff said. This provoked several of the others to laugh.

"You keep an eye peeled fer 'im. Don't go tanglin' with 'im neither. He's a killer." The sheriff waved to his men and got the ragtag bunch riding back along the arroyo in the direction opposite that taken by Consuela and Don Rodrigo. Again, Slocum thanked his lucky stars. He ought to let Consuela and her crazy brother find their own way back to Mexico, but somehow he felt he had to warn them.

Then there was the lure of El Loco being the actual robber who had stolen twenty thousand dollars' worth of gold.

Getting a share of that would go a long way toward paying him back for all the trouble he had run into since having his horse shot out from under him.

It took the better part of the day for him to be sure he had found their trail on the hard ground. He kept looking over his shoulder to be certain the sheriff wasn't following, but even if the lawman was an expert tracker, those with him were greenhorns. Slocum knew he would have spotted anyone on his trail long before he was sure he had picked up the hoofprints from Consuela's horse.

She and her brother had headed due east, then slowly circled and headed northward on a trail parallel to the main road into Eagle Pass. Slocum wished the sheriff had been more forthcoming with information about the stolen gold, but learning of it had been a start. Slocum knew if he had been too curious, the sheriff might have poked around the campsite more and possibly found that there had been three, not one, spending the night in the arroyo.

Only an occasional glance at the ground kept him on their trail. From the stride shown by the indistinct markings in the sand, they traveled fast. Slocum wondered why they had sneaked out of camp the way they had and where they went in such a hurry. He found travel increasingly difficult due to the lack of water. His head spun a mite, but not enough to warn him to go to ground until dark. He hoped they only had a few hours head start on him and that he could overtake them before sundown. The thirst building in his mouth and throat, though, quickly put the lie to any hope he had of overtaking them.

When he realized he wobbled in the saddle, Slocum found himself some dubious shade under a mesquite bush and let his horse eke out what she could at a greasewood bush, about the only two plants other than cactus that seemed to grow in this stretch of West Texas desert.

Slocum half slept, half passed out, and came to when

the sun dipped low. The chill gave him the energy to go on, but he walked his mare. She needed water as badly as he did.

As he put one boot in front of the other, he turned over in his mind all he knew of El Loco. The man might be responsible for the gold theft, though it seemed unlikely. Maybe the heat had driven him even crazier in the past month, or he might have had lucid stretches where he could plan and pull off a robbery. The notion that Don Rodrigo had simply been riding out in the desert, seen the opportunity, and taken it to steal the gold was far-fetched.

Slocum snorted at the idea of anything that happened to El Loco as being far-fetched. The man blew through the countryside like a whirling dust devil, kicking up sand and stones and moving erratically. With him, anything was possible.

"Gotcha," Slocum said, dropping to his knees and studying the imprints he found in the dirt and rocks. Consuela and Don Rodrigo had stopped here for some time. He found the woman's footprints as well as her brother's.

Even better, he found a canteen that had been tossed aside. He pounced on it and pulled the cork to let a trickle of precious water drain into his mouth. It wasn't much, only a few ounces, but it revived him.

He sat back and ran his tongue over his cracked lips to capture even the memory of the water. Then he began wondering why either of them had dropped a canteen with even a drop of water inside.

No matter how crazy Don Rodrigo might be, he wasn't going to throw away water in the desert.

Slocum heaved himself to his feet and began a closer study of the tracks. He had to piece together much of what he saw because the ground didn't take kindly to tracks. Changing his tactics by spiraling outward caused him to stare. Twenty yards off he found hoofprints from several horses. Dropping to his hands and knees to get a better look convinced Slocum that Consuela and Don Rodrigo had spotted at least half a dozen riders.

With this information, he reconstructed what must have happened. Consuela and Rodrigo had stopped to drink. One of them had spotted the riders, it had frightened them enough that one had dropped the canteen, and the two of them had ridden away in different directions. Slocum tried to figure out which track to follow. He cared more about Consuela than he did Don Rodrigo. Or did he? The lure of the man knowing where a large gold shipment was hidden drew Slocum. Divvying it up would go a long way toward making his travel through West Texas profitable.

Getting shot at and losing a horse was regrettable, but it would be made a lot more palatable with that much gold weighing down a pack mule.

Unable to decide which tracks belonged to Consuela, he chose the ones most likely to have been followed by the host of riders. Less than a half mile away, Slocum saw where the gang had gone after a lone rider. It hardly mattered who it was. If he tracked Consuela, he could save her. If the prints were left by Don Rodrigo, he could find out where the gold was stashed—assuming El Loco knew anything at all about the robbery. More than once, his crazy boasting had gotten him into trouble. Slocum had to believe this might be the case again.

"Shoot your mouth off and you might get your damned fool head shot off," Slocum muttered as he rode. Following the trail became more difficult when the sun began dropping behind the mountains at his back. He would have felt better about this if Don Rodrigo had headed for the Rio Grande and the uncertain safety of his home on the far side.

Slocum had to get a better hold on his fantasies. He might be after Consuela instead of her brother. His taste for gold was growing too strong to let the chance of finding it slip through his fingers. But it might.

He drew rein when he saw curls of smoke rising ahead, caught by the setting sun and turned into bloody columns reaching for the sky. A quick look around told him getting near the fire would be hard. Whoever had lit it camped in a shallow ravine. If he was right about the number in the gang, at least one would be walking guard duty. The flat land prevented him from riding much closer.

Throwing his reins around a creosote bush limb, he settled down to wait for darkness to enfold the land. A chilly breeze kicked up from the direction of the fire. The scent of roasting meat and coffee brewing made his mouth water and his belly rumble. It had been too long since he had a decent meal—or even a good swig of water.

He forced himself not to stir until a sliver of moon came up over the horizon. He judged it to be waxing to a quarter moon, giving plenty of light for him to see by but not enough to betray him as he approached the camp. As much as he hated to admit it, the fire might have been lit by someone honest going about his business. Even in West Texas, this wasn't too far-fetched a notion.

Keeping low, he advanced until he came within ten yards of the campfire. To his right, he heard spurs jingling. Sinking belly down on the ground, he resisted groaning as spines from a cactus pod cut into him. He watched a sentry walk within a few feet. The man's face was hidden in shadow, but Slocum had the feeling he knew him as one of Duke Denham's gang.

The outlaw passed by without so much as a glance down in Slocum's direction. It took a great deal of patience for Slocum to force himself to lie still a few more minutes. When he rose to a sitting position, he plucked at the nettles cutting into his chest and belly until they no longer distracted him. A few more yards forward allowed him to peer down into the shallow ravine. Two campfires burned low. One held the coffeepot and the other a spit where a rabbit roasted. Again, hunger and thirst hit him like a hammer blow.

Then he saw Duke Denham. The outlaw leader strutted about, pointing and kicking but saying little. A step behind walked Luther, who acted as his boss's voice.

"Duke says for you to get out. He wants two guards, just to be on the safe side."

"Ah, Luther—" began an outlaw. Duke Denham kicked him hard in the side. The man reacted, hand moving toward his six-shooter. He stopped when he stared down the barrel of Denham's six-gun. Denham was fast, but Slocum knew he was faster.

"It's Duke you outta be addressin', not me," Luther said. "Just 'cuz he can't talk since—" It was Luther's turn to clam up. Denham spun on him and croaked something incoherent but obviously vicious. "Sorry, boss. We'll catch that son of a bitch for you." Luther cleared his throat and spoke again to his cohort. "The boss said he wants it known *he's* still in charge. I'm only his lieutenant."

"Got it," the outlaw on the ground said. "Lemme get out onto guard duty right now." He struggled to his feet and took a few unsteady steps. Slocum knew he had been drinking. As the man slipped away, Slocum eased back to avoid being seen. He need not have worried since the man was in such a hurry to get away from Duke Denham.

"Where is the she-devil?" Denham's voice came as a rasping whisper, but to Slocum's ears it might have been a shout.

Throwing caution to the wind, Slocum moved back to a spot where he could look into the camp. Denham faced Luther and shoved his face within inches to make himself heard.

"We got her tied down over yonder, out from underfoot."

Slocum could see only one spot. A lone mesquite grew in the middle of the wash. Under it he made out a dark form.

"Will she talk?"

"We'll make her, boss. You know we got ways." Luther grinned broadly as he drew a knife and brandished it.

Slocum fought against his impulse to draw and start shooting. Luther and Duke Denham would be the first to die, but there were too many others. If shooting began, he would come out as a loser.

Him and Consuela.

12

Slocum slipped away from the camp, but he stopped after a few yards and crouched down behind a low drift of sand to think. He could not leave Consuela in Denham's hands. There was no telling what the outlaw had done to her already, but Slocum knew what the son of a bitch would do if he had her any longer. Slocum had been drawn into this mess by the lure of gold. The thought of twenty thousand dollars in gold coins was almost more than he could pass up.

But Don Rodrigo knew where the gold was, not Consuela. Slocum tried to tell himself he was going back into Denham's camp to rescue Consuela because she could lead him to Don Rodrigo and convince her brother to split the gold. Slocum knew that was close to being a lie. He was going to save Consuela because it was the right thing to do. Such thinking only led to death, but he ignored that.

As he started to stand, ready to go scout the camp, he heard a muffled curse. He froze, but he was in the wrong position, all twisted and unable to move easily. A charley horse caused his right thigh to seize up and send him crashing to the ground with a moan. This was all it took for the guard to come to investigate.

"Who's that?"

"Me," Slocum grated out, rubbing his knotted leg to ease the pain in the muscle. "Takin' a dump."

"Who are you?"

The guard incautiously stepped closer, his rifle still resting in the crook of his left arm. He outlined himself against the rising moon so that Slocum had a better target. With a quick grab and toss, Slocum picked up a rock and hurled it. There wasn't enough force behind the rock to do real damage, but the guard flinched.

"Since when was any of us so modest?" The guard rubbed his cheek where the rock had struck him. "I'm gonna pound yer head in." He came forward again, but still did not have the rifle leveled.

Slocum got to his feet, but his right leg was still knotted in pain. He swung clumsily, missed, and almost fell. This was enough for the guard to see that he had an intruder on his hands.

"Hey, fellas, o'er here!"

Slocum stayed on his knees, but this time fell forward and tackled the man around the ankles, bringing him down in a heap. Not giving him a chance, Slocum swarmed up and punched hard three times. One of the blows knocked the guard out.

"Whatcha goin' on about, Brandon?" The voice came from some distance away.

"Got any booze?" Slocum tried to duplicate the guard's voice, but he was a terrible mimic and had not heard enough to fool anyone. Luckily, the answering guard was the drunkard who had staggered from camp.

"Ain't sharin' with the like of you!"

"Go to hell," Slocum muttered, knowing some response was better than none at all. The last thing he wanted was for the other guard to get suspicious. He rolled away from the first guard and tended the spasm in his leg. It slowly relaxed. By the time Slocum stood without wobbling, the guard he had knocked out was coming to.

"Wha—?"

Slocum considered the stakes. Consuela's honor and her very life were on the line. He might shoot his way out, but more would die. He drew his knife and plunged it into the semiconscious guard's chest before he could rouse the rest of the outlaws.

Panting as much from emotion as effort, Slocum cleaned his knife and sheathed it in his boot before slowly moving away. If they found the dead guard, they might get spooked and leave in a hurry. More likely, Denham would rouse everyone and send them out to avenge the dead man. Either way afforded Slocum no chance to rescue Consuela. Stealth was his only ally.

He moved as quickly away from the other guard as he could. His leg still cramped, and he didn't want to put more strain on it than necessary. Slocum circled the camp and dropped into the ravine on the far side of the mesquite tree where Consuela was tied. Using sound to guide him more than sight, he edged closer to the tree. A low moan told him he was close.

Wiggling on his belly, he worked around the mesquite and reached out to touch Consuela. He hesitated and that saved his life. The dark form stirred, growled deep and long, and sat up.

Slocum stared at a back far too broad to be Consuela's.

"What's goin' on?" the bear of a man grumbled.

"We're movin' our lovely li'l visitor, that's what. Come on over. We can take turns." An outlaw near the campfire moved, and for an instant was fully revealed to Slocum in the light. Slocum didn't know the man, but saw that he held a bound and gagged Consuela too firmly for her to even struggle.

The man he had thought to be Consuela got to his feet and lumbered off. Slocum sank down and tried to look like part of the rocky ravine bottom. Everyone in camp was up and moving around now. It wouldn't take much for them to spot him if he moved—and he couldn't lie where he was much longer. The moon poked up over the rim of the arroyo, casting its pale silvery light everywhere. If he tried to retreat, he would be spotted, and if he stayed, he would be seen, too.

Moving slower than molasses on a winter day, he edged for the dubious shelter of the mesquite tree. When he got behind it, the delicate leaves and sharp, thorny branches kept him from being seen by anyone in the camp. That was small consolation if the roving guard happened on him from the other direction.

"We gonna have some fun with her, Duke?"

Slocum couldn't hear the gang leader's response. From the discontent that passed through the tight knot of outlaws, though, the answer had not pleased them. Slocum had been wondering if Duke Denham wanted Consuela for something else other than a little rape. He knew now that he wanted what her brother had hidden. The gold would buy a lot more pleasure from whores than a single roll in the hay with Consuela. He wanted her to lead him to Don Rodrigo.

Slocum hoped she knew what would happen then if she cooperated.

All he heard were muffled cries as she tried to speak around her gag.

Another idea hit him. Denham might be keeping Consuela gagged to prevent her from telling anyone else where Don Rodrigo rode. He might want the information for himself so he could deal the rest of his gang out of the treasure.

"Now, you boys know the boss ain't gonna just let her go. There'll be plenny of time with her for us all," said Luther. This produced some grumbles, but most of the gang approved of waiting to rape her rather than taking turns now.

Slocum chanced a look, and saw that Consuela had been dragged away to the far side of the ravine and might not have heard this vow. She was clever and had to know nothing Duke Denham promised was likely to be honored. If she took him to her brother, both brother and sister would be dead when the gold was unearthed.

He found himself in the same position he had been in earlier. He could tangle with the lot of them and die, or he could try again to rescue her by sneaking around and waiting for when she only had a single guard. Slocum berated himself for thinking that anyone separated from the main group was likely to be their prisoner. Why the outlaw had come out to sleep under the mesquite was a question Slocum didn't bother thinking on. It mattered more that Slocum get the hell away.

After ten minutes, the outlaws had settled down a bit, but none had curled up in his bedroll. They sat around the campfire, drinking coffee and swapping lies. Slocum worried more and more about the guard along the arroyo bank. He might be half drunk, but if he found his dead partner, he'd sober up mighty fast.

Knowing he had no choice, Slocum stood, took a deep breath, and began walking slowly toward the spot where the ravine bank had caved in. Every step took him closer, but the middle of his back began to itch with an imagined bullet tearing into him from behind. He almost collapsed with relief when he got to the bank and found sanctuary in the deep shadows. The men around the campfire had not noticed him, or if they had, they had figured he was one of the gang. He had taken a risk walking slowly rather than making a dash, but it had worked.

He scrambled up the bank and got his bearings. Consuela was on the far side of the ravine. Getting into position to rescue her was out of the question now with the entire gang between them.

Slocum went for his six-shooter when he heard the drunk guard let out a screech.

"Brandon's been kilt! Something knifed him! Get your asses out here now!"

All hell was loose now.

Slocum scrambled and got his feet under him, but his leg throbbed fiercely. He rubbed it as he stumbled along, angling away from the outlaws' campsite and heading for his horse. For a few minutes, he thought luck was with him. Then Lady Luck turned fickle.

"There he is!"

A rifle spat angrily in his direction. The bullet went wide but Slocum ducked, caught his toe, and fell hard to the ground. In pain, he forced himself back up. By now two rifles were firing wildly. They knew his general location, and that was good enough to make it dangerous to run. If he wanted to find that posse and bring back the sheriff, he had to get away without too many ounces of lead in him.

If he returned fire, he knew he would make more of a target since they could sight in on his muzzle flash. Slocum turned and hobbled directly away from the outlaws. Their firing became sporadic, and he heard Duke Denham's grating half voice ordering them to stop. As the firing died down, Slocum kept going as far as he could, but when the last round had come in his direction, he dropped to his hands and knees and waited.

Any sound now would alert them.

"You sure that ain't just a coyote that spooked you?" asked Luther.

"Brandon! He got his danged throat slit!"

"Naw," said another outlaw. "The knife went into his belly. But no coyote did that to him, 'less they're all carryin' steel out here."

Luther began barking orders. If Slocum had a partner, this would be the time to send him in to save Consuela. Barring that, Slocum had only one mission: save his own life.

Moving cautiously on all fours, he kept low out of the moonlight and appeared more like a coyote. He heard two men coming up behind him, but they veered away and vanished into the dark. Slocum hurried now, getting to his feet and limping along the best he could. When he reached his horse, stepping up into the saddle proved quite a chore. His right leg refused to swing up and over, so he flopped belly down over the saddle and spun until he could get a good seat.

His mare was nervous, but he kept her quiet until he had walked her a hundred yards. Only then did he start up to a quick trot. In the dark, he didn't want the horse to step into a prairie dog hole and break a leg, but staying near the outlaws' camp was just as dangerous.

When he was sure he had ridden far enough, he slowed, got his bearing by the moon and stars, and tried to guess where the sheriff and his posse might have ridden in their hunt for Rodrigo. They were his only hope of rescuing Consuela. The cavalry patrolled out here endlessly searching for the Apaches, but the chances of accidentally crossing paths with a cavalry patrol were so small, Slocum did not even consider it.

What he should have considered was the reason the cavalry sent endless patrols into the West Texas desert.

"This isn't my night," he said softly, patting the mare's neck. Lady Luck had turned into a real bitch. Slowly riding in single file in front of him was an Apache raiding party. He recognized the way they slouched along with eyes to the ground, the silent step of their horses, and the speed of their passage. Moonlight glinted off rifle barrels and bits of silver and turquoise jewelry adorning the warriors' headbands.

One by one, he counted them until he came to fifteen. This was a good-sized party and one that definitely needed the attention an entire company of cavalry. But Slocum had found the braves, not the U.S. Army.

He sat as silent as a statue, watching them pass. A plan churned in the back of his mind, fighting to boil to the surface. He had a wild idea, and immediately rejected it as foolhardy. Then he found himself with no other option. The guard trailing the main body spotted him.

Slocum drew and fired an instant before the Apache. Neither round came close to its target, but the sudden reports alerted the others. The Apache who had fired at Slocum yelled a warning. Slocum kept firing in the direction of the man's voice. Then all he could do was wheel about, duck low, and ride like the wind.

His horse strained under him, but it was rested from his long excursion into Denham's camp and the relatively easy ride to escape. Now it strained and flew through the air, devouring distance under flashing hooves.

The Apaches did not let out war whoops because they had no idea what they faced, but they came after him. He heard their ponies galloping along, but they were tired from long, forced marches and having to elude the cavalry with nighttime retreats. Slocum put more and more distance between himself and the Apache raiders, but the idea that he had rejected before now seemed the only way out.

He could have ridden away at an angle to Denham's camp. Instead, he rode directly for it. Slocum fumbled to reload his Colt, and considered drawing the Winchester for the actual approach to the outlaw campsite. It came too fast for him to switch weapons. One instant he was galloping over the desert, and the next he rode along the crumbling arroyo embankment. Down below, several outlaws jumped to their feet and began firing. Slocum's elevation and aim were better. He winged one man and sent him crashing to the ground amid a barrage of curses.

This was the best he was likely to accomplish. Slocum turned his horse and rode directly back toward the Apaches, firing until his six-shooter came up empty. Once more, he reversed direction. This time the Indians were so close he imagined he felt their hot breaths on his neck.

The mare came to the rim of the arroyo at a dead run. She jumped out and into the arroyo. Slocum kept going, scrambling up the far side and then turning toward the spot where he hoped Consuela was still being held.

Now he drew his rifle. He didn't trust himself to dismount and advance on foot. His leg throbbed like a bad tooth and could give way under him if he put too much weight on it. From horseback he began firing, not down into the outlaws, but across the sandy gulch into the attacking Apaches.

Outlaws and Indians collided in a furious exchange of gunfire that occupied both sides completely.

Slocum slid off his horse and dropped to the ground. His fears were well founded about what he could and could not do. Barely walking, he got to the edge of the arroyo and hunted for Consuela.

The fight kept Denham and his gang busy, but again Slocum had mistaken one of the outlaws for Consuela. The spot where he thought she was being held captive showed only a man as skinny as a rail clutching a rifle.

Slocum raised his Winchester and fired at the same instant as the outlaw.

Hot pain lanced through Slocum's leg, and he fell forward into the arroyo.

13

Slocum hit the ground hard. The impact jarred him, but he hung on to consciousness with a grim determination born of knowing he was a dead man if he passed out. He rolled to his side and brought up his rifle. The scrawny outlaw who had shot him wasn't looking in his direction. Slocum read the man's lips.

"Injuns!"

This distraction was all Slocum needed to squeeze the trigger on his rifle. The recoil knocked the weapon from his feeble grasp, but the bullet flew straight and true. The outlaw threw up his hands and died on the spot. Slocum grabbed for his Winchester and used it as a crutch to stand. He was shaken up and his leg hurt like a million ants were gnawing on it.

"Why gang up on me like that?" he wondered aloud. The leg that had seized up with the charley horse now had a deep, bloody crease, too. Slocum went to the dead outlaw and took his six-gun. The need for firepower would become critical soon enough. He heard the Apache war cries and the fusillade that met them. If he hadn't stirred up Denham's camp earlier, the Apaches would have struck and found them asleep in their bedrolls. He wasn't sure who he was cheering on in the pitched battle raging on the other side of the arroyo.

Every step he took was pure pain, but Slocum forced himself to keep moving, hunting for Consuela, trying to keep his head down as the bullets flew.

For whatever reason, the battle died down. He heard Luther shouting orders to get the outlaws into a defensive position. At the same time, he saw a guard pacing nervously, waving his six-shooter around, and looking ineffectual. Slocum made his way toward the outlaw because he also saw a small body huddled at the man's feet.

"Consuela?"

He called the woman's name and got a sharp reaction from the indistinct shape on the ground. The outlaw spun about, bringing up his pistol. Both Slocum and the outlaw fired at the same time. Slocum's aim was better. The man yelped as he jerked back, Slocum's bullet raking along his forearm and forcing him to drop his six-gun.

"Back off," Slocum said, not wanting to cut the man down unless he had to. "The Apaches are going to overrun your camp. Go tell Denham."

"Who're you?"

"Run!" Slocum lifted his Colt, and would have shot the man if he hadn't lit out like a scalded dog. He waited a few seconds to be sure the outlaw wasn't going to return, then dropped beside Consuela. Tears ran down the woman's cheeks, leaving muddy tracks behind. He pulled the gag from her mouth.

"John, you came for me. I thought I would never see you again."

"That makes two of us," Slocum said, drawing his knife to cut the ropes on her wrists and ankles. "Can you walk?"

"Of course I can walk, oh!" Consuela stumbled and fell to her knees. "My feet are numb. They are brutes and tied me too tightly."

He used the rifle as a crutch to support himself with one

hand, and reached around the woman's shoulders to support her. Together, they staggered along, going away from the gunfight that was heating up again. When they reached the far bank, Slocum's strength gave out and he collapsed.

"You are wounded," Consuela said, seeing his bloody leg for the first time. "I did not know. Here, I have been leaning on you."

"We have to get the hell away from here," Slocum said. "I'm not going to bleed to death from this." The leg actually felt worse from the muscle spasms than the gunshot wound.

"My horse is with the others." Consuela looked around, then pointed. "There is the corral. They tied their horses to a rope strung between two creosote bushes." A bullet kicked up a small dust cloud just above their heads. Slocum noticed. Consuela didn't.

"Get your horse and meet me up on the bank. Can you do it?"

"I think so. What if I see one of Denham's gang?"

Slocum pulled the captured six-gun from his belt and handed it to her. He had known it would come in handy. Getting rid of hardware was never a good idea, but now they were both armed.

She gripped the heavy gun in both hands, then nodded once to let him know she would use it if necessary. She gave him a quick kiss and a smile that promised him everything, then hurried off to fetch her horse. Slocum watched her fade into the darkness, then heaved himself upright. It took more strength getting to the arroyo rim. When he succeeded, he turned and dropped to sit with his legs dangling over the edge so he could figure out how the fight was going.

It was too much to hope both sides would be wiped out. From the way some men were suddenly outlined by muzzle flashes and others dashed about, he separated the attacking Apaches from the defending outlaws. Luther had rallied the men and passed along Denham's orders well. They were slowly taking their toll on the Indians and prevailing.

Slocum knew it was time to hightail it.

"That way," Slocum said, turning his horse in the direction he wanted Consuela to ride. He raked his spurs along the mare's flanks and took off at a gallop. It was dangerous running through the desert like this, but it was more dangerous staying back in the outlaw camp waiting to see who won the pitched battle. From the last glimpse he had of the fight, Duke Denham would come out the victor and the Apaches, those remaining, would creep away when they realized no one was going to pursue them.

After a few minutes, Slocum slowed the pace and looked over his shoulder. Consuela rode along, a grim, determined expression on her face. When she came alongside, he slowed and finally stopped to give their horses a rest.

"What the hell happened?" he asked.

"You know more than I do," she said, looking around. The determination had been replaced by fright now. "Apaches, Denham, so many are after us!"

"This morning. Why did you and Rodrigo leave without telling me?"

She licked her lips and looked away. The words came slowly.

"He rode off. I feared your anger. He is a good man, my brother, but he is loco. I thought I could persuade him to return so you could escort us across the Rio Grande."

"Denham grabbed you?"

"The one named Luther," she said. "They did not harm me. They wanted to use me to force Rodrigo to return, but he was already . . . somewhere else."

Slocum started to ask if she knew about her brother and the gold shipment, then held back. Sometimes, playing his cards close to the vest worked best. There was always time to ask if she knew about how tangled up Don Rodrigo was in the gold theft.

"They tied me and took me to the camp where you found me. When I called out too often, they gagged me."

"Where's Don Rodrigo?"

The abrupt question shocked her. Slocum had hoped it would bring out the truth without her thinking about it too much.

"I . . . I do not know."

"He's roamed all around the country and has to know it pretty well. Is there someplace he might hole up? Someplace he'd feel safe?"

"I don't know."

"Why do you think he really left like he did?"

Consuela shrugged her shoulders and said apologetically, "He is not called El Loco for nothing. He needs care. If he stays in this country much longer, he will be harmed."

"Killed," Slocum said. "I ran into a posse hunting for him after his antics in Chupadero Springs." He held back telling her what he had learned from the sheriff. Instead, he said, "He must have done some mighty big damage for the county to send out a posse that big."

"County? A sheriff is after him?"

"As well as Marshal Atkinson and the folks from Eagle Pass and Duke Denham. If you count us into the hunt, he's got damned near everyone on his trail since the Apaches will kill any white eyes they find. Where would he go?"

"Closer to the river, I suppose," she said. Consuela did not sound convinced, and neither was Slocum.

Before he said another word, he sat a little straighter and turned his head so he could listen to hoofbeats coming from the direction of the outlaw camp.

"We've got somebody on our trail," he said. "Unless I miss my guess, that's Duke Denham and his men. They were coming out on top of the fight with the Indians. It's taken him this long to find that you weren't still in camp."

"We must go!"

"Not so fast," Slocum said, reaching over and grabbing her bridle to keep her from running off willy-nilly. "Our horses are tired after their gallop. We can't push them much farther without them dying under us."

"Water," she said, her voice shrill. "Rodrigo would hunt for water. We must also."

"First, we've got to get away from Denham. Tracking at night is hard and doing it in this desert is even harder. One of his men must have seen us leave the camp in this direction." He pointed off to rising sand dunes to their right. "We can get some cover that way. If Denham rides straight as an arrow, he'll miss us."

"The soft sand will slow our horses and tire them quickly," Consuela said.

"It'll also go a ways toward hiding our tracks." Slocum dropped from the saddle, and almost fell when his leg protested the weight placed on it. Using his knife, he hacked at some greasewood branches. He took a few more minutes looping his lariat around the clump of vegetation he had cut, then tied the end of the rope to his saddle horn.

Without another word, he motioned for Consuela to precede him. He followed, dragging the brush to cover what little tracks they did leave. They entered the sand drift area, and Slocum saw that Consuela was right. The horses struggled to walk in it. Fort Davis had experimented with camels before the war, but they had not worked well due to the extensive rocky patches that broke their hooves. Still, he wished he was on one of the oddly shaped beasts now to get as far away from the outlaws as possible.

He kept them moving due north after their initial ride to the west. Doubling back appealed to him, but only if their horses had been rested would such a trick work. They would be sitting ducks if they rode exhausted horses and one of Denham's men spotted them.

"I am tired, John, and my horse is, too. We must rest. *I* must rest."

"Keep moving," Slocum said. He hadn't heard any pursuit since they had moved into the sandier areas of the desert, but he doubted Denham would give up easily if he thought the only way to find the stolen gold lay in using Consuela as a lever with Don Rodrigo. He would track her to the ends of the earth.

"John, I cannot keep going. Neither can you."

Slocum felt woozy, and knew he had almost fallen from the saddle a couple times, but he knew their only hope was to keep moving. The horses were stumbling in the soft sand, but he knew Denham would be scouring the land for them. If they stayed in the deep valleys between the wind-driven sand dunes, they avoided being seen by any of his scouts, but this patch of desert was quickly turning rocky. Slocum knew they would be out on the flats again where anyone on horseback could see for miles.

"We need to find someplace to go to ground," he said. The mountains to the west were appealing and offered any number of hiding places, but reaching them was going to be a problem. It was almost dawn and the mountains were miles off. The first time he had ridden through the desert, he had been fooled by the apparent nearness of places. Those mountains might be a hard day's ride off. Or more.

"Water," she insisted. "We must find water."

"I don't know the watering holes," Slocum said, "but there's one way of finding them." He motioned for her to get off her horse. He stepped down and gingerly put weight on his leg. The muscle cramp was a distant memory, but the bullet wound sent a lance of pain into him every time he stepped. Reaching up, he held on to his pommel for support. It was an awkward way to walk, but he could do it.

"We rest the horses," Consuela said, "but it does nothing to find water. We would see vegetation better if we stayed in the saddle."

"Give your horse its head. If it smells water anywhere within miles, it'll go to it."

Consuela looked doubtful, but loosened her grip on the reins. It lifted its head and snorted loudly. Its nostrils flared, and then it set off in the direction Slocum wanted to go anyway. The mountains were a haven for him. He had hunted and trapped and lived in mountains since coming west from Georgia, and knew the ways of those piles of rock. He and Consuela could reach what he took to be the Anacacho Mountains—or were those farther to the north? His brain was fuzzy with fatigue and pain and no water.

"The horse is rearing," she said, trying to hang on to the reins.

"Let it go."

"What if it runs away?"

"We're not going to be that much worse off, are we?"

She started to argue, but her horse wrenched free and trotted away purposefully. Slocum had no trouble getting his mare to follow. What he did find difficult was hanging on so he could walk and keeping the horse from breaking into a gait too fast for him.

Consuela walked behind, muttering to herself.

"Keep on this side of the greasewood," he said, although the brush had been almost entirely rubbed down to twigs.

"It is stupid. They do not follow."

"Denham has worked as a road agent in this area for a while. He might know where the watering holes are. He could be on his way here, no matter if he's lost our trail. I don't want him to pick it back up."

"You worry so," she said. "At times you sound like Rodrigo."

Slocum wondered how he could respond to that. Was he completely loco like her brother, or was the lack of water doing it to him?

His horse reared and caused him to lose his grip on the pommel. The mare totted away faster than he could walk. Consuela hurried up to help him.

"I see trees ahead. Do you think there might be water?"

"You mean, did my cockeyed scheme work?" He began laughing when he saw that it had. The horses pressed close to each other as they drank from a small pool of water, only now reflecting the first rays of morning off the rippling surface. With Consuela's help, he made his way closer and looked around for animal carcasses that might show this to be an alkali spring. He saw no telltale sulfur patches on the rocks or anything else that might mean this wasn't pure water.

He dropped to his knees and began scooping the deliciously cool, wonderfully wet water into his mouth.

"Sweet water," he murmured. No wine or whiskey had ever tasted better.

"We will not die of thirst," Consuela said, plunging her head entirely beneath the surface. She came up sputtering and laughing, her long dark hair plastered to her head from the immersion. "You are a miracle worker, John Slocum. *Este es un milagro!*"

He washed his face, then tended the wound on his leg. It burned like hell when he washed away the dried blood and dirt that had caked the shallow groove in his flesh, but after applying a bandage made from strips torn from Consuela's skirt, he was able to walk about with little pain.

"I'll be good as new in a few days," he said.

He filled his canteens and let the horses have another deep drink before he pulled them back. They looked a little bloaty to him, but they deserved the water after getting him and Consuela away safely.

"We can stay here and rest," Consuela said. She batted her eyes at him and pulled down the water-soaked neckline of her blouse to expose the tops of her delightful breasts. "Or we can rest after we—"

Slocum put his finger to his lips. He turned and looked along their back trail. His hand flashed for his six-shooter when he spotted Luther and Duke Denham riding toward the watering hole.

14

"We can't fight them all," Slocum said, keeping his hand on the ebony butt of his six-gun but not drawing. His mind raced to find a way out of this pickle. "Get up anything we might have dropped and stash it."

While Consuela worked to retrieve their gear, he took a branch from a cottonwood tree and worked to erase their hoofprints and footprints. It was a piss-poor job, but Slocum didn't have the time to do a more thorough job. He hoped that the pale light of dawn would hide what he couldn't.

"Come on," he said, grabbing his mare's reins and leading the horse away. The mare tried to rear, but Slocum held her down. Consuela followed, looking at him with great concern etched on her face.

"We cannot hide from them. They will see us. And there is no way we can ride away without being seen."

"I know," Slocum said, hobbling as fast as he could. His leg felt as if he had thrust it into a campfire until it burned constantly, but he kept moving because he had to. He headed for a second small grove of trees some distance away. There might be another spring bubbling up there, and if so, he had to keep going. Denham and his gang would check every source of water in the area.

Behind, he heard Luther barking orders to his men. Slocum itched to take his rifle and go back, lie in wait, and make a couple of killing shots at the outlaws. If he drilled both Duke Denham and Luther, the rest might lose heart and run off. Such a notion was nothing more than wishful thinking, however, and he knew it. He led his horse through the thin grove and out the far side. He looked around for someplace to hide. There was nothing but flat land stretching away from this tiny oasis. If they tried to gallop off, they would be heard. Any slower pace and they would run the risk of being seen.

"We make our stand here," he said, handing Consuela his horse's reins. Slocum pulled his Winchester from the saddle sheath and found a spot where he might take a pot-shot at any rider approaching this grove.

"We cannot stay here, John. They will see us."

"I've had such bad luck so far, it's got to turn." He knew that was not too realistic. He had seen runs of bad luck during card games that lasted for hours. Just when he thought it wasn't possible to get a worse hand, he'd get it. Sometimes that came from the dealer stacking the deck, but other times it was simply rotten luck.

"Check that other grove," boomed Luther's voice. Slocum thought he heard a raspy command that would come from Denham, but he could not be sure. He rested the rifle against a tree trunk and drew a bead on the outlaw trotting over.

"Never mind. Get yer ass on back here," Luther shouted. "They can't be too far ahead of us, if they even came this way. Don't see that they did, but we need to drink up and be on our way real quick."

Slocum kept his Winchester aimed at the outlaw's back as he rejoined the rest of the gang around the watering hole. He let out a sigh of relief when he heard horses slurping up water and the outlaws sloshing around in the small pool.

"They will find us," Consuela said glumly. "They are not blind."

"Might be they're in a hurry," Slocum said. "The sooner they find you, the sooner they can find your brother." He waited to see if she would volunteer anything about the gold shipment and El Loco's involvement. When she didn't, Slocum knew he had to get Consuela and Don Rodrigo together before broaching the subject. He could play one off against the other that way.

"They are leaving," she said, heaving a deep sigh of relief. "Do you think they will return?"

"They'll head straight for the river," Slocum said. He tried to visualize the lay of the land. What struck him most was how the desert opened up hot and flat and went directly westward to the Rio Grande. If Duke Denham wanted to run them down, he would hurry to prevent them from reaching the sanctuary of the far side of the river.

He considered checking to be sure that the outlaw leader hadn't left a guard at the watering hole. If Slocum were in Denham's place, he would do that very thing. Maybe more than one would watch to see who showed up. After their run-in with the Apache raiders, the road agents would be warier of their back trail.

"What do we do?"

He looked at the lovely woman and knew with a sinking certainty where her brother had gone.

"Eagle Pass," he said.

"I am so tired, John. Can we rest?"

Slocum almost relented because he ached all over, too. They had been lucky finding another watering hole. The water carried the bitter tang of alkali, but had been drinkable because they were so thirsty. The two days of riding away from the watering hole where Denham had almost caught them seemed more like two months. The only good thing coming from their ride was the way his leg felt better. The bullet wound had begun to heal and walking no longer sent stabs of pain into his hip.

He didn't hurt, but he did ache. Bad. Real bad.

"There's a spot of shade," he said, knowing how wrong it was to give in to weakness. The ground had turned rockier here, giving some hope they were nearing the main road from San Antonio up to El Paso. Along that Butterfield route lay Eagle Pass and Fort Davis and other towns. The vegetation looked more like that around Eagle Pass, but the road remained elusive. Slocum realized his inability to find something so prominent cutting through the desert was due to the punishment the sun had meted out to him, making every second an eternity. He wasn't anywhere near as sharp as he had been, and his mind drifted more and more as the heat mounted.

They had to rest.

"Enough shade for us," Consuela said, nodding. She turned her exhausted horse toward the vegetation growing along a high embankment. It was late enough in the afternoon that shadows crept over the fiery landscape.

Slocum dismounted, felt a twinge, and then led his horse to a spot where he could tether the mare in the shade. He took off the saddle and received a heartfelt neigh of relief as thanks.

He spread his bedroll and dropped, using the saddle as a pillow. He stared up into the cloudless blue sky, and had started to drift off into a troubled sleep when he heard Consuela moving closer. He turned and saw her kneeling a few feet away. Before he could say anything, she spoke.

"I want to thank you, John. You have done so much for me. For Rodrigo." She began undressing, peeling off her blouse from her sweaty body until she was naked to the waist. Slocum was tired and wanted to sleep, but the sight of her breasts gently swaying as she moved toward him was delightfully hypnotic.

She lifted her skirt and showed brown thighs as she straddled his waist.

"Do nothing. I will do it all for you."

"You don't have to . . ." His resolve faded when she reached down and pressed into the mound growing at his crotch. He was getting harder by the instant just staring at her. Her nipples were hard little brown pebbles, showing her own arousal. Slocum moaned softly as she unbuttoned him and let his manhood spring out. Her nimble fingers circled his hardness and began moving up and down slowly until his balls tightened with need.

She knew exactly how best to excite him. Her fingers slid downward to the base of his shaft and guided it as she positioned her hips above him. Then she sank down and took him slowly, warmly, all the way into her tightness.

Slocum gasped as he felt her all around him. Reaching up, he pressed his palms into her breasts. She put her hands atop his and silently implored him to shove down even harder. He didn't need the urging. His fingers opened so he could capture her nipples between them. He began squeezing down as he felt the distant throb of her excited heart.

"Oh, yes, John. I need this so."

Her hips began swinging from side to side, back and forth, up and down while he was still trapped within her. He hardened even more at this rotary motion. He tried to give her as much pleasure as she was giving him, but wasn't sure that was possible. The warmth from her inner core spread downward into his body, through his loins, and then throughout his body. His breathing came faster. Slocum stroked over her sleek body, tracing the large breasts capped with the hard points of her nipples, then downward, across her belly, around to her back where he touched each and every bone in her spine as she bent forward.

Their mouths touched, teasingly, lightly, then in a kiss so hot it rivaled the sun beating down on the West Texas desert. Consuela began rising and falling slowly, taking him full length into her body and then slowly letting him slip free.

They continued the kissing and fondling and slow lovemaking for as long as they could. Then neither could hold back. Slocum arched upward to drive in deeper as Consuela lowered her hips. She ground herself down hard into him and finally exploded in a frenzy of motion. The carnal friction mounted and Slocum was soon lost. He tried to drive himself as far into her yearning interior as possible— and she tried to take him. She let out a tiny shuddery gasp and then sank forward, her cheek against his.

"Oh, John, if only this could be the way always," she said.

He held her for a while, and then she slipped away to sit beside him. Consuela looked out across the heat-shimmery desert.

"This is a cruel land," she said. "I want to return to Mexico."

"Is it any better there?"

"It is green where we live. There is a large valley with grass and cattle grazing. The vaqueros work the herds and there is so much prosperity."

"Not enough for Don Rodrigo," Slocum said.

"No, never for him. He is loco," Consuela said sadly. "He must be watched constantly."

"You can't spend your entire life looking after your brother."

Consuela shrugged her bare shoulders and turned slightly toward him. He saw how sad she was.

He reached to her and drew her close so she could put her cheek on his chest. Slocum felt her warm, steady breathing and the hot tears. Finding Don Rodrigo and getting the information out of him about the gold shipment just got a little harder.

Just a little.

"Why should Rodrigo return to Eagle Pass?" she asked. They sat astride their horses at the southern edge of the town.

From what Slocum could tell, nothing had changed since he had left, not that he expected anything to be different. Towns like this grew by leaps and bounds, and disappeared as suddenly, when fueled by mining. Eagle Pass existed only as a center for ranches and as a stopover for the Butterfield Stage Company. When the railroad was built joining San Antonio and Mesilla, Eagle Pass would dry up and blow away unless the tracks passed close by, but until something catastrophic like that happened, the town would just . . . exist.

"He can go home to Mexico. Is that what he'd do?" asked Slocum.

"No, he is having too much fun in Texas," she said with a touch of bitterness in her words. "He is going to be killed."

"Most likely, unless we find him before Denham does."

"And the others. There are others in Eagle Pass who would harm him. They laughed at him, now they would hang him."

Slocum had nothing to say about that since everything Consuela said was true. Don Rodrigo had not left town on a good note. The likeliest notion Slocum could come up with was that Luther had framed him for shooting a cowboy in the back so he could get more men out hunting for Don Rodrigo. That situation wasn't likely to have resolved itself.

"Was there anyone in town he would consider a friend?"

"No one. They gave him drinks so he would perform like a trained dog. They were not his friends." She turned, her dark eyes on him. "You were as close to being his friend as anyone in Eagle Pass ever was."

Slocum regretted having intervened and taken on Duke Denham and his entire gang, but it might pay off handsomely if he found Don Rodrigo and learned what he knew of the stolen gold.

"You go to your room," he said. "Or would it have been rented already?"

"I will see. If it has, I will wait for you behind the boardinghouse while you carouse."

"I need to check the saloons and you'd give the wrong idea if you went with me."

"I am not *una puta*," she said with distaste. Little by little, he felt her hostility and anger toward the town and people of Eagle Pass growing. Part of it transferred to him, but Slocum hardly blamed her. She and her brother had not been treated well, but a lot of that had been caused by El Loco's own actions.

He watched her ride off, leading his horse. She made a pretty sight, sitting astride her saddle. He felt a pang down low as he remembered how good it had felt when she had ridden him out in the desert. That had been reward enough for what he was doing, but Slocum wanted more. The smell of gold made his nostrils flare and his heart race. More than once, he had been on the wrong side of the law, and had robbed a stage and a bank or two along his winding trail through the West. Finding Don Rodrigo's shipment and keeping it—or at least splitting it with El Loco and his sister—was only fair payment for all he had done since coming to Eagle Pass.

The crowd was gathering in the Hijinx Saloon, so he went in. He tried to make himself blend into the crowd, but the barkeep spotted him right away.

"Hey, ever'body. Slocum's back!"

He put up with several customers at the bar buying him drinks and slapping him on the back as if he were a long-lost brother. Or at least an uncle. Slocum tried to poke and prod to get what he could from them about Rodrigo, but they pointedly ignored his questions.

When the novelty of his return wore off, he found himself sitting at a table at the rear of the bar, drinking alone. This suited him because he could watch everyone in the saloon and even eavesdrop on some of the nearby conversations. It took him only a few minutes to realize the bonhomie had been a facade and that everyone in the room was terrified of something.

When a drunk staggered past his table, Slocum thrust out his boot. The man fell heavily. Slocum hastily helped him up.

"Sorry, old-timer. I didn't see you. Here, have a drink." Slocum poured, and the man used two hands to keep from spilling the whiskey in his haste to down it. The man looked expectantly at Slocum, who obliged by pouring another. "Why don't you join me?"

The man eyed what remained in the bottle, and looked around as if a hawk would swoop down and steal away his newfound source of booze. Slocum kicked out a chair and waited. It took only seconds before the man collapsed and pulled the bottle to him. A furtive look told Slocum the man was considering running away with the bottle.

"Help yourself. Here. Use this." Slocum pushed his own shot glass over, and the drunk eyed it suspiciously. Slocum almost read his mind. Downing the liquor shot by shot wasn't fast enough when all he had to do was upend the bottle, open his throat, and let it all gush down into his gullet.

"You're a prince among men, Slocum," the man slurred.

"Tell me what's been going on around town since I left. Hasn't been long since I rode out, but people seem different."

"M-marshal's outta town. Out huntin' fer him."

"Him?"

"El Loco." The man hiccuped and then belched loudly before taking another drink. He laughed. "Joke's on him."

"Why's the joke on Marshal Atkinson?"

The drunk leaned closer and breathed on Slocum. That fierce gust would take paint off boards.

"He's here, that's why."

"El Loco's in town?"

"Shush. Don't say that. Don't mention him. H-he'll kill you, he will. Been threatenin' ever'one with that six-shooter of his. Been right mean to ever'one fer all they done to him."

"The posse—"

"He run 'em off. All of 'em."

Slocum found this hard to swallow. Still, he wasn't out more than a few shots of whiskey for a man willing to talk when others clammed up, no matter how roundabout he was in his questions.

"He rode into town and whoosh! They was all gone. The marshal's out huntin' fer somethin'. Don't know what, but he don't know El Loco's back. Mark my words. Gonna be blood in the street when he gets back."

"Where's El Loco now?"

"He hangs out at the edge of town, at the bakery. You kin tell how crazy he is. He sits there sniffin' the air when they're bakin' bread. Looks like a damn fool." The drunk clapped his hand over his mouth. "He'd kill me fer sure if he heard that."

"Drink up," Slocum said, pressing the bottle into the man's hands. He saw the looks on the others' faces as he left. They knew where El Loco hung out, too, but were too chickenshit to even speak about it. How a crazy vaquero had cowed them was a marvel.

All Slocum could think as he strode to the far side of town was how lucky Don Rodrigo had been that Luther or Denham hadn't returned to Eagle Pass. Luther had put up a sizable reward. Somehow, Rodrigo had made trying to collect the reward less appealing. Slocum wondered why someone hadn't tried shooting El Loco in the back, then remembered Luther's reward had been for a live and kicking prisoner, not a corpse. That had to put the townspeople in a terrible bind. They were afraid of El Loco, but couldn't kill him without losing the reward.

"You. Halt! There! Halt where you stand!"

Slocum saw El Loco shoot out of a chair propped against the bakery wall and come storming into the middle of the street. Don Rodrigo squared off and went into a gunfighter's crouch, hand ready to go for his six-shooter.

"I'm going to take you to your sister." Slocum watched Rodrigo. The man's hand was steady and his eyes were hidden under the broad brim of his sombrero. What he was thinking was a mystery. That made him all the more dangerous. Slocum couldn't get it out of his head how Don Rodrigo had blasted a crow to hell and gone back in Chupadero Springs with a single shot. That might have been a lucky shot, but Slocum didn't want to take the chance that Rodrigo wasn't a crack shot.

From the way he stood poised to draw, Slocum couldn't say whether the Mexican was able to drag out that smoke wagon of his in a lightning-fast move or not.

"You will not do this," Don Rodrigo said. "I am El Terrible! I am the fastest gunman in all the West."

"Not disputing that," Slocum said slowly. "Consuela wants to talk to you. You can talk to your own sister, can't you?"

"This is no place for women."

Slocum almost asked about the gold, but held off when he heard loud shouts behind him. He chanced a glance over his shoulder, and knew trouble had boiled over in Eagle Pass. The drunk must have spilled his guts about everything he had said to Slocum and provoked the rest of the saloon patrons to come out. They had forgotten their cowardice and remembered their greed.

"You've been causing a lot of woe in town, Don Rodrigo," Slocum said. "They're coming after you for making them look small."

"They are nothing! They cowered before me!"

Slocum wondered if the six-gun was loaded. Taking the chance that it wasn't seemed a bad bet from the set to Don Rodrigo's body and the way he focused.

"We can't stay here. They're fed up with you pushing them around and threatening their lives," Slocum said. He felt a growing desperation as he heard the drunken crowd and what they were saying. They had finally imbibed enough Dutch courage to go after Don Rodrigo. The money Luther had offered the small posse was an inducement, but whatever

Rodrigo had done since coming back to town had had them all too afraid to face him.

Until now.

"I will show them how masterful I am. I am the fastest gunfighter in the whole West!"

"It'd be my honor to stand beside El Terrible," Slocum said. This produced the response he had hoped for. Rodrigo came out of his gunfighter's crouch and looked at ease. He might have been complimenting Slocum on his impeccable taste, to judge by the size of the smile Rodrigo bestowed on him.

Slocum advanced cautiously, and turned when he reached a spot beside and just behind Don Rodrigo. The crowd was gathering and hunting now.

"We will show them what real men can do!" El Loco went for his pistol. Slocum was faster. He slid his Colt Navy from its holster and swung it hard, landing on the side of Rodrigo's head. El Loco dropped to the ground in a boneless heap.

Slocum stuffed his six-shooter back into his holster, added Don Rodrigo's to his belt, and then grunted as he dragged him off the street. The crowd hadn't spotted them yet. Yet. They would scour the town. They would see anyone riding out. A million problems surged through Slocum's head, and then he knew the only spot where Rodrigo would never be found.

Favoring his hurt leg but dragging Don Rodrigo as fast as he could, Slocum headed for the jailhouse.

15

"In jail! You put him in the jail!" Consuela's dark eyes widened and she stepped away from Slocum. Her hands came up and balled into fists as if she wanted to hit him.

"Don't get all mad," Slocum said.

"You put him in *jail!*"

"For his own good. The men in the saloon finally got some backbone and decided to lynch him."

"So you put him where they could find him? I trusted you, John. I thought you were trying to help. I did not know all you wanted was the reward on his head."

Slocum snorted. It wasn't much of a reward. Luther had offered fifty dollars. There might be more from Chupadero Springs, where Don Rodrigo had caused such a stir with his crazy ways. Slocum didn't even want to think of all the others, lawmen and otherwise, who might be hunting for the man. The sheriff and his posse wanted the gold shipment—and so did Slocum.

"He's safe there," Slocum said. "Would anybody in a drunken mob ever think about looking for him there?"

This stopped Consuela. Her hands relaxed, but the suspicion in her eyes remained. She reached out and put her palm against his chest, as if checking to see if his heart was still beating.

"You do not turn him over to the marshal?"

"I don't know when Atkinson will be back, but Rodrigo won't be in the calaboose when he does return. I'll see to that."

"He would be out getting into trouble if he were not behind bars," Consuela said, slowly seeing the genius of Slocum's plan. "I must assure him all is fine."

"Come on, but get your horse ready. Mine, too. I don't know where your brother's is, but we're likely to have to sneak out at a minute's notice. The crowd won't find him, and eventually will go back to the saloon to brag on how brave they are. A few drinks past that lie and we can leave."

"I'll meet you at the jail. Be careful."

Slocum almost asked her about what Rodrigo knew of the stolen Butterfield shipment, but held back. She might not realize Rodrigo was the key to finding twenty thousand dollars worth of gold. As Slocum returned to the jailhouse, he reasoned that El Loco might know nothing about any stolen gold and had only shot off his mouth in Duke Denham's hearing. The outlaw leader wasn't too bright, and the notion of stealing gold that had already been stolen would draw him like a fly going to fresh cow flop.

Slocum paused at the side of the jail, looking all around to see if anyone noticed him. The crowd that had gathered in front of the Hijinx Saloon was already dispersing as small knots of men hunted for El Loco. None of them even looked in the direction of the jail. After all, who would hide inside a jail when a lynch mob was after you and the marshal was out of town?

Slocum smiled as he slipped inside and closed the door behind him. The jail office was cool and dim and a relief from the burning sun outside. He went to the rear and looked in on his prisoner.

El Loco sat on the bunk, staring hard at a bare wall.

"Where is it?" Slocum asked.

"My soul is imprisoned. How can I hold up my head proudly like the hacienda owner and vaquero that I am?"

"How did you learn about the stolen gold?"

Don Rodrigo shook his head, but Slocum couldn't tell what the man responded to. It might have been the question or more rumination on his sorry state being locked up in a jail.

"Consuela will be here soon," Slocum said.

"She is a dear girl. *Mi hermana*," said Rodrigo. "She deserves more than I give her."

"Is that why you stole the gold?"

"I have much gold. More than any man can count in a lifetime. Two lifetimes! I am rich beyond the dreams of mere Texans."

Slocum started to ask where he could find some of these riches when he heard the outer door rattle. He drew his six-gun and went to the doorway leading into the office. He lowered his pistol when Consuela slipped in. For a moment, he wondered if he had ever seen a more beautiful woman. She was silhouetted by the bright sun outside and, as she turned sideways, he saw the fullness of her figure and her fine facial features. Then the door closed and she half vanished in the dim interior, lit only by cracks in the door and a few crevices high on the ceiling.

"He is here?"

"Right back in the cell," Slocum said. She pushed past him and went to her brother. They spoke in such rapid Spanish that Slocum was left far behind. Mostly, Consuela chided Rodrigo for being so stupid and pretending he was El Terrible, a famous gunman and outlaw. Slocum listened for anything that might tell him about the gold shipment, but nothing obvious was said. Leaving them to their talk, he went into the office and sank into the marshal's chair. It threatened to give way under his weight, just as it had under Marshal Atkinson's bulk.

He closed his eyes and tried to think of ways to find out
about the stolen gold. Duke Denham might have been blowing smoke, coming after Don Rodrigo because he thought
the vaquero knew something about the missing shipment,
but Slocum didn't think so. Denham was something of a
failure at robbing stages, but he was tough enough and smart
enough to know not to chase the wrong scent. The scent of
gold was particularly strong to men both honest and otherwise. And the sheriff had said a gold shipment had disappeared, the guards killed. The Apaches weren't likely to
steal gold. They'd steal the horses and leave everything else
behind.

A gringo—or a Mexican—had hidden the gold. Everything pointed to Don Rodrigo as the answer to the burning
question of where the gold was.

Slocum didn't bother thinking about his place among all
those who were after Don Rodrigo. The thieving had been
done. All he intended to do was find the gold, maybe take a
share, and move on. The owners, whoever they might have
been, already considered the gold lost. Why shouldn't he
get some use from something that most reasonable men had
stopped hunting for?

"John?"

His eyes snapped open to see Consuela standing in front
of him. He was more tired than he thought, drifting off that
way.

"Anything wrong?"

"No, nothing much. It is just that my brother is hungry.
He has not eaten in a day or longer."

"My belly's rumbling, too," Slocum said. He had found
water in water barrels outside and drunk some of it, but had
neglected to eat. "Why don't you go fetch something for
the lot of us?"

"You'll watch Rodrigo?"

"Of course," Slocum said, thinking he could use the
time alone with the vaquero to question him more about

what he knew. El Loco might have seen something and not known it. His wild fantasies could have taken him anywhere and made him do anything, though Slocum doubted he had robbed the gold shipment by himself. More likely, he had seen the robbery and knew where the gold had been stashed.

"I will not be long," Consuela said, taking the pair of greenbacks Slocum gave her. The bills were soaked with sweat after riding in his vest pocket so long, but the ink hadn't smeared much. It was still good money, at least in Eagle Pass. The woman left. Slocum made sure the latch was in place before securing the handle with a loop of rawhide Marshal Atkinson had used to lock the door.

Slocum spent the next ten minutes trying to pry any hint of what Don Rodrigo might know from him, but the man was lost in his fantasies of being a rich hacienda owner and running thousands of head of cattle.

Slocum hoped Rodrigo didn't get this fantasy confused with the one about being a gunfighter. Otherwise, there would be dead beeves everywhere.

"That's your sister bringing back some food," Slocum said when a soft tap came to the jailhouse door.

"Tortillas," Rodrigo said. "I like tortillas. I hope she has brought some. And frijoles. Some *carne adovada* also."

Slocum left Rodrigo itemizing all the things he enjoyed eating and went to the door. He slipped off the rawhide loop and swung the door open a fraction to look out. That was the last thing he remembered until he regained consciousness a few minutes later.

He sat up and rubbed his forehead. The lightest touch made him wince, and his fingers came away sticky with blood. His head still spun, but piecing together what had happened wasn't too hard. Consuela had knocked, he had opened the door, and—

"Don Rodrigo!"

Slocum swung around and got his feet under him. He

took a quick look in the rear of the jail and saw the cell door standing wide open.

"Son of a bitch!" He returned to the outer door and opened it, hand resting on the butt of his pistol. The sun was setting and left a bloody light amid lengthening shadows behind. He looked up the street toward town, but saw only what he'd expected. Men were coming in from the surrounding ranches for another night of drinking and forgetting about their sorry lives. Nowhere did he see Rodrigo or Consuela. By now, he realized Consuela had had no reason to slug him, so that meant someone else had. They had either let Rodrigo go free or had taken him prisoner.

"Denham," he muttered. The name came out as a curse.

He went around behind the jailhouse and saw that both Consuela and Rodrigo's horses were gone. His mare remained, nervously pawing at the dirt and rearing when he approached.

"Where'd they go? Where did Denham take them?" he asked the horse. Not getting an answer, nor expecting one, he swung into the saddle and rode into the main street. No one paid him any mind as he trotted the length of the town. He kept his eyes peeled for any trace of brother and sister or the Denham gang. It was as if they had evaporated from the earth like some fog in the morning sun.

"It's got to be Denham," he said. This was the only explanation that made sense to his throbbing head.

"How's that, Slocum?" A man had come out of the Hijinx Saloon and clung to the porch support.

"You see El Loco or the pretty señorita with him?" Slocum asked the drunk who had told him about Don Rodrigo's antics. The man belched and tried to hang on tighter to the support. He spiraled around and ended up sitting on the edge of the boardwalk.

"I seen three, four men ridin' outta town a few minutes back."

"Which way'd they go?"

The drunk thought about it, looked north, and pointed, but his finger swung about past Slocum and ended up like a faulty compass needle pointing southward.

"Thataway," he said. "I think. Mighta been some other way, but I don't think it was."

Slocum wanted to beat the truth out of the man, but knew that wouldn't make the answer any more reliable. If anything, it might change simply because the drunk would want Slocum to leave him be.

"Much obliged," Slocum said, putting his spurs to his horse's flanks. He galloped off, slowing when he reached the edge of town. The road was all cut up from traffic throughout the day, but he hoped to find a fresh track or two before the sun disappeared entirely behind the distant horizon.

Slocum had to dismount and press his cheek against the ground to get a better view of the ridges and depressions alongside the road before he convinced himself a half dozen or more riders had come this way recently.

It took him a second to stand when his leg refused to move right. He rubbed it and felt the pain receding. He needed to lie low for a few days and recuperate, but there was not going to be a chance anytime soon. He felt an obligation to Consuela to rescue her from Duke Denham and his gang. Then there was Don Rodrigo and what he knew about a missing gold shipment.

Even if Denham killed Consuela and Rodrigo, there might be a chance to steal the gold away from the outlaw when he went to fetch it. That would be cold comfort for Consuela and her brother, but Slocum wasn't going to let Denham ride off with the gold after killing them. He heaved a sigh as he stepped up into the saddle. He wanted to stop Denham from killing anyone else. The gold would be reward enough for that.

As he rode along, following the ghost trail, he became downright morose. There might not even be any gold. The sheriff and his posse roaming the West Texas desert might have it all wrong. Considering how Marshal Atkinson acted, along with the fine citizens of Eagle Pass, jumping to conclusions was a local sport with too many participants.

After reaching the crest of a low rise and staring out over the now night-shrouded desert, Slocum knew he was not going to be following Denham until dawn. That might be for the best, but he hated letting the outlaw get that much of a start on him. The riders seemed to be heading toward low mountains some distance off. He debated the merits of heading in that direction against stopping and waiting for morning, when he could find their trail and continue. He had no idea of Denham's ultimate destination. Don Rodrigo could have spilled his guts and told the outlaw where the stolen gold was hidden.

Slocum rode for the mountains. If he were Denham, a hideout there would be what he would seek out. A couple of guards on ridges would give ample warning of an approaching posse. Or Indians.

He reined back when he saw the silhouette of a warrior riding ahead. Slocum touched his six-shooter, but did not draw when he saw four more riders. It was unusual for Apaches to travel at night, but the cavalry was kicking up all kinds of fuss and might have flushed them from wherever they had camped. And the other night he had run into a band that he had lured into attacking Denham and his gang in order to free Consuela.

The lead rider pointed ahead and let out a coyote call. This caused Slocum to sit a bit straighter in the saddle. They not only hunted something—someone—but they had found that someone or something.

The only others likely to be in this stretch of lonesome desert were Denham, his gang, and his prisoners.

Slocum waited ten minutes until the Apaches rode off in the direction of the mountains. He was glad he hadn't passed them sooner, or they would have been on his ass. Even if they weren't after Denham, staying behind the Indians was smarter than anything else he might do, other than giving up and returning to Eagle Pass.

He stayed off the ridges, but the Apaches traveled them to get a better look at their quarry. A few words drifted back that Slocum understood. "Enemy" was mentioned several times, but not the way the Apaches would speak of the cavalry. They held a grudging admiration for the buffalo soldiers and their officers, even as they did their best to kill them.

Slocum worried about what to do if the Apaches overtook Denham's gang and captured Consuela and Don Rodrigo. More likely, they would kill Rodrigo, but they would use Consuela for some time before killing her. It was a long, dusty, dangerous trail for the Indians after they had left the Warm Sands Reservation, and they would take whatever pleasure—revenge—they could as they passed through West Texas.

An earsplitting battle cry rang out. The actual coyotes in the distance fell silent, and the usual sounds of the desert at night all quieted. Even the wind chose to pause as if to listen. The pounding hoofbeats following the challenge told Slocum the Apaches had found their enemies and were trying to spook them.

If that was the reason for the war cry, it didn't work. Rifle fire came almost immediately. A few shrieks of pain followed, but Slocum wasn't in any position to tell what was going on.

He balanced his chances of surviving, and decided they were poor if he insinuated himself between two angry, armed groups in the middle of a nighttime battle. Both sides would shoot at anything moving in front of them, and Slocum would fit the bill for both outlaw and Indian.

But he couldn't simply remain idle while Consuela was in danger. He urged his skittish mare to a fast walk and headed west toward the river. When he had gone a mile or so, he turned back toward the battle, angling in to come upon the fighters from a direction he hoped would not spur instant retaliation.

The shots had died down somewhat, but sporadic reports warned him how dangerous it still was. Knowing he couldn't just ride up, he dropped from the saddle, caught himself as his leg gave way, then found a place to tether his mare. From there, he advanced on foot. He clung to his rifle as if it were his lifeline. More than once, he had to use it as a crutch to get up a steep, sandy slope. When he heard horses nearby, he went to ground and slithered up like a snake to peer over the crest of a sand dune.

He wasn't sure what he was looking at. Dark shapes lay scattered all around, but determining if they were outlaws or Indians wasn't possible. In the distance a horse cried out in fear. A single gunshot followed and the horse's cries ceased. Then there was nothing but a fitful wind blowing across the sandy spit where the fight had occurred.

Slocum watched for several minutes, but saw nothing moving below. He worked his way down the face of the sand dune and then got to his feet. Limping heavily, he reached the first body. He recognized the outlaw as one of Denham's gang. Not ten feet away sprawled an Apache brave filled full of holes. Slocum couldn't tell, but it looked as if he had been shot six or seven times, and even this many slugs might not have stopped him until the round that had entered his left temple and exited his right found him.

Quickly working through the dead, Slocum found six Apaches and four outlaws. He doubted there had been many more Indians than this. Denham's men might have killed every last one of them. As he prowled around more, he decided that Denham knew he was being tracked and had laid an ambush. That almost as many of his men had died as Apaches was a testament to how fiercely the Indians fought.

Or it might have been a badly laid trap. Slocum couldn't tell. Nor could he tell where Consuela and Rodrigo were.

He looked around, and wearily retraced his steps to where his mare nervously waited.

"We've got a bit more riding to do," Slocum said, patting the horse's neck, "but there aren't as many of them left for us to shoot."

The horse took no consolation in this, and neither did Slocum.

16

Slocum didn't want to do it, but felt he had to. He waited until dawn before following Denham's gang into the hilly country. The trail was difficult to see, but more than this, he didn't want to run afoul of more Apaches or any trap Denham might set for those coming after him. Slocum wished he could have determined if the dead Indians were part of the same raiding party he had lured into Denham's camp before, but he couldn't. There must have been a strong thread of revenge holding the Apaches on the outlaws' trail after that massacre.

Slocum shook his head in wonder. A no-account outlaw like Duke Denham was doing the cavalry's work for them. The horse soldiers hunted high and low for the Apaches and found damned few of them, resorting instead to laying ambushes at watering holes to fight them. Denham had only to ride through the countryside and draw the Apaches to him like ants to a Sunday picnic. Even better, he killed them. Slocum doubted Denham was in line for any medal, though, after trying to rob the Butterfield stage at least twice and probably committing all kinds of petty robberies wherever he alighted.

The trail was plain enough for a blind man to follow,

and that worried Slocum. There wasn't any reason for Denham to hightail it like he was doing if he thought all the Apaches were dead. He had to know that neither Marshal Atkinson nor the sheriff from down Chupadero Springs way was after him. The only explanation Slocum could come up with was that Don Rodrigo had spilled his guts and Denham was on the way to digging up the stolen gold.

If he were in Denham's boots, he would be galloping hell-bent for leather for the gold, too. The yellow metal was too powerful a lure not to hook anyone. Nobody need be on his trail for him to want to hurry to get his hands on the gold.

An hour after sunrise, Slocum drew rein and looked around. He saw no one, but his gut churned in worry. Listening to such warnings had served him well during the war, though he had not seen Bloody Bill Anderson's bullet to his belly coming. He had been too mad at William Quantrill to realize that his own life was in danger. Quantrill's Raiders had gone into Lawrence, Kansas, with orders to slaughter any male over the age of eight. Anderson and too many of the others had pushed that age down lower. Slocum had done his share of killing, but murdering unarmed boys, no matter how good Quantrill considered his reasons, was where Slocum drew the line.

He drew the line, and Quantrill ordered his most bloodthirsty henchman to remove Slocum.

Slocum thought that if he had kept his head about him, he would have seen Anderson coming and not ended up gut-shot and an invalid for long months afterward. Right now, his sixth sense told him something was wrong.

He tilted his head back and looked into the cloudless blue sky. Tiny dots circled far above. Buzzards. Something big had died, and the hungry scavengers were waiting for the coyotes and smaller animals to finish with the carcass before coming down to claim their share.

Fearing what he would find, Slocum left the trail and

rode a dozen yards to one side. The buzzing of flies warned him of the first body. His heart jumped into his throat when he saw Don Rodrigo's sombrero covering the face of the dead man. He dropped to the ground and pulled off the broad-brimmed hat. Whoever had died, it was not El Loco. Slocum rolled him onto his side and saw the outlaw had been shot in the back.

Backing away, he looked around for some clue about what had occurred here. As far as he could tell, the man had fallen from his horse after being shot once. Slocum kept the sombrero and went back to his horse, where he hung the hat over his saddlebags. He had started to mount when he heard movement from behind. He slipped back to the ground and drew his six-shooter as he turned.

A coyote peered around a creosote bush at him, fangs showing and yellow eyes glaring in hatred. When the animal took a step toward him, he lifted his pistol and fired a single shot. The coyote rose on its hind legs, then keeled over, dead. The bullet had ripped directly into its mouth and tore down its throat. From the sound of feet hitting the sunbaked ground, Slocum knew he had disturbed a pack of the scavengers.

Cautiously rounding the bush, he saw another body. This one had been mostly eaten by the coyotes and was probably drawing the most attention from the buzzards aloft. The other body hadn't been dead long enough to begin to spoil in the hot sun.

He examined the second body the best he could, and found the spot in the middle of the back, right over the spine, where a bullet had entered. Both men had been murdered by someone riding behind them. Slocum wondered if El Loco might have gotten his gun loaded and swung into action. The Mexican was something of a marksman, and could easily have drilled both outlaws smack in the middle of their backs as they rode, but was he the killer? Slocum had no evidence one way or the other.

The dead men's horses might have galloped away, or they might have been taken by the rest of the gang.

Slocum pursed his lips as he considered this. How many of Duke Denham's gang remained in the saddle? The Apaches had taken a few with them to the happy hunting ground. Slocum had looked for Luther's body and had not found it, but that didn't mean he wasn't already dead. Truth was, it meant nothing at all. Denham and his right-hand man might be herding Consuela and Don Rodrigo to wherever the gold had been hidden. If so, two more lives wouldn't be worth spit when the shipment was unearthed.

Leaving both bodies untouched since he was unwilling to take time to bury the outlaws, Slocum rode back along the trail, eyes on the hills rising ahead of him. The early morning light lit them with a ruddy hue that made the rocks look as if they had been dipped in blood. He rode a little faster at the thought of how that blood just might be Consuela's, but kept a keen eye out for any hint of ambush. He worried it might be one of Denham's traps and was a little edgy as he found a game trail leading steeply upward into the hills.

More than an hour later, Slocum came onto a road that appeared to wind up from the Rio Grande. He didn't have to dismount to see that a heavily laden wagon had followed this ancient road recently. His heart beat faster. The only wagon likely to be coming up this way into uninhabited mountains dotted with deserted mines was the one carrying stolen gold.

When the mare balked, Slocum gentled her and cocked his head to one side. The sounds drifting down from higher in the hills were hauntingly familiar, but he had a hard time placing them. Then he listened more closely. Someone was digging. He heard a shovel grind into dirt and rock and then the load being dumped onto the ground. When it came again with the precision of a machine, he knew someone worked steadily burying something.

Or digging it up.

He stayed on the road for another half mile, then dismounted to advance on foot when the road took a sharp turn around a bend leading into a canyon mouth. Slocum drew his six-shooter and edged forward until he could see down the canyon. Not twenty yards away, Duke Denham sat on a rock with his rifle trained on El Loco. Don Rodrigo made the sounds Slocum had heard, shovel driving into loose dirt and then discarding it. From the heaping pile behind the vaquero, he had been working for some time.

Slocum moved to keep out of Denham's line of sight, but he hardly needed to worry. The outlaw's attention was fixed entirely on Don Rodrigo and the outline of a wagon he was unearthing with every shovelful of removed dirt. When Slocum was in a decent position in a cluster of rocks not ten yards behind Denham, he settled down. He could see Rodrigo past Denham, but barely. This put the vaquero in the line of fire, but Slocum knew he wouldn't miss Denham if he had to shoot.

In a way, as diligently as Rodrigo worked, Slocum was almost hypnotized. The dirt slowly vanished as the side of the wagon took form. From the look of it, the road agents had driven the wagon close to an embankment, then used dynamite to bring down tons of dirt to cover it. Slocum wondered if they had intended coming up here to hide their loot right from the beginning.

And if they had, what had gone wrong with their plan?

"Keep diggin'," came Denham's hoarse whisper. "You almost got it all out. You done good."

Don Rodrigo made some reply that Slocum couldn't catch. Slocum stood up and peered past Denham to get a better look at the vaquero digging so aggressively at the buried wagon, and then forced himself to look away. Where was Consuela? The woman was nowhere to be seen. If he rescued Don Rodrigo, he had better be damned sure he wasn't also killing Consuela.

"I'll cut you in, if you tell me the rest of your secret."

This caused Slocum to perk up and listen harder. He had permanently damaged the outlaw's voice box if the man was still talking in a raspy whisper. Denham would be out for revenge—but what else? Something Don Rodrigo knew and had yet to tell the outlaw was on the table. It might be all that was keeping the vaquero alive now that the wagon was exposed to the light of day again.

"I do not know what you mean," Rodrigo said. He swiped his arm across his face and kept digging.

"You surely do. You said you saw them. How far off? How many?"

"I know nothing more to tell you. This is the gold."

"Looks to be, but you got to tell me what you saw."

Slocum lifted his six-gun, getting ready to plug Denham in the back if he had to. The outlaw was getting angry that Don Rodrigo wasn't more forthcoming with whatever morsel of information he was holding back. Slocum wondered if Rodrigo knew where Consuela was and the outlaw didn't. He aimed directly at Denham's back, his finger coming back slowly. If this was the case, he could kill Denham, get the gold, and find out from Don Rodrigo where his sister was. If Denham didn't know, that had to mean she had escaped and was safe somewhere in the foothills.

"It is done," Rodrigo said, throwing down his shovel. He tossed his head back and let loose with the most bloodcurdling cry Slocum had ever heard. Then he began dancing around wildly, waving his arms and whooping and hollering like an Apache at a war dance.

"Stop it. Shut up or I'll kill you!" Denham sighted down his rifle. Slocum's finger tensed for the kill, but Denham wasn't going to fire. He was only trying to quiet El Loco's outcries.

"I will dance, I will sing. I am a troubadour of the finest kind. None in all of Mexico sings love songs better than I!"

El Loco spun and whirled and kicked up a small dust devil at his feet as he performed in ways never seen by any other man. Not content, he broke into a song in Spanish that Slocum knew was bawdy but whose lyrics were a mystery to him.

"They'll find us, damn you. Shut up!" Denham slid down the rock and was momentarily out of Slocum's line of sight. When the outlaw reappeared, he swung his rifle barrel and struck Don Rodrigo on the side of the head. The vaquero went down heavily. He no longer danced, but even this mistreatment couldn't stop his singing.

Denham muttered angrily under his breath, kicked Rodrigo, and then went to the rear of the wagon to begin pawing through the loose dirt remaining in the bed. Slocum inched closer, hand sweating on the butt of his Colt. Rodrigo's off-key singing masked any sound Slocum might make as he crept within a few yards before slipping behind the boulder where Denham had perched just minutes before. From there he had a clear enough field of fire to get a clear shot at the outlaw.

"Son of a bitch," Denham rasped out. "Son of a bitch! This *is* the gold. All of it, just waitin' for me to take it." He laid his rifle down in the wagon bed and grabbed the strongbox with both hands to pull it free from the dirt still partially burying it. With a grunt, he yanked the box free and slid it to the edge of the wagon. Slocum moved to where he could get a better shot, but he still hesitated.

Denham reached for the rifle, but he was too intent on the gold to hear any sound Slocum might make. El Loco saw Slocum and stopped singing. Slocum put his finger to his lips to keep the man silent, but it didn't work. Rodrigo laughed loudly and began a heated debate with himself in Spanish. Denham ignored the man entirely as he lifted his rifle and used the stock to hammer at the lock.

The metal hasp broke and the lock swung free. Denham

dropped his rifle again and threw open the lid. He laughed louder and wilder than Rodrigo as he ran his fingers through the gold coins inside.

Slocum reckoned it was time for him to act. He stepped out, but before he could say a word, a shot rang out. Duke Denham stood bolt upright, half turned, a confused expression on his face. Then he sank to the ground, dead.

Slocum whirled about, but kept from firing when he saw Consuela a few feet behind him, a rifle to her shoulder.

17

Slocum and Consuela stared at each other, saying nothing. She didn't lower her rifle, but he did holster his six-shooter. A smile came to her lips.

"You are persistent, John. I should have expected you would not give up so easily."

"I don't take kindly to being slugged the way I was back in Eagle Pass."

She lowered the rifle a little, but he noticed how she still kept it aimed in his general direction.

"Put down the rifle," he said. "You got Denham. It's all over."

"Who hit you in town?"

"You're the one who'd have to tell me." Slocum tensed when she lifted the rifle a little in surprise at his question.

"Why do you say that?"

"You had to have been seen when you went to get food for your brother. One of Denham's men followed you and hit me when I opened the jailhouse door. But you must have been their prisoner by then."

"I was," she said, finally pointing the rifle at the ground. She heaved a huge sigh of relief. Slocum found himself distracted by the way her blouse draped open from a long tear that started on her shoulder and went across her left breast. Enough tantalizing flesh was revealed to make his mind wander to more exciting times with her.

"What did they do to you?" He pointed to her ripped blouse.

"It was terrible. That is why I killed him. He will never do such a terrible thing to anyone ever again."

"You're as good a marksman as your brother."

"What is in the wagon?"

Slocum started to speak, then thought better of it. He waited to see if Don Rodrigo piped up with an answer, but the man sat cross-legged in the dirt next to Denham and sang some little ditty in Spanish that made no sense to Slocum.

"Reckon we ought to see," Slocum finally said. "Denham was all fired up over what was in the wagon." He turned and gestured for her to go ahead of him. Consuela hesitated.

"I am sorry, John," she said, brushing past him in such a way that her naked breast rubbed along his chest. "I have been through so much. It has shaken me so much I can hardly believe it is all over."

Slocum watched as she went to the strongbox and reached in. She let the gold coins trickle through her fingers the same way Denham had. And Slocum saw another similarity. The fire of greed burned brightly in Consuela's dark eyes.

"You knew what was in the box," he said. "You knew your brother would lead Denham here."

"I lied, John," she said.

"About what?"

"Oh," she said, turning and starting to aim her rifle in his direction. "Everything."

He cleared leather and had her dead to rights, but did not pull the trigger. Slocum's hand shook the barest amount. He tried to believe that came from too little food and sleep, but knew he was lying to himself. Gunning down Consuela wasn't something he could do easily after all they had been through together.

"You're the one who hit me back in Eagle Pass," he said.

"Of course I am. You knew that from the moment you rode up. I can tell these things."

"Sister, what's going on?" Don Rodrigo looked up at Consuela with wide eyes and an expression that told of complete insanity.

"Nothing, *pendejo*," she snapped. "I have put up with you too long. Always you get into trouble I must rescue you from. I am sick of being nursemaid to you. I will never be free—unless I take this gold for my own!"

"I want to go back to my hacienda."

"That's right," she said, a sneer on her lovely lips. "*Your* hacienda. Not mine. Never mine. You keep me like a slave, a servant to wipe your chin of drool. You are *muy rico*, but I eat with the peasants in the kitchen."

"It's a big hacienda," El Loco said.

"He really owns a spread in Mexico?" This startled Slocum more than anything else Consuela had told him.

"More than a hundred thousand acres. Many thousands of head of cattle. He is the richest man in all of Coahuila— and he acts like an idiot. He *is* an idiot, a fool!"

Slocum glanced down at Don Rodrigo. He had gone along with using the honorific because it had been what Rodrigo had expected. Slocum wondered now if Consuela was the crazy one.

"No," she said, spitting. "I am not crazy. My brother is." She kicked him. He rolled onto his side and made animal noises. "He never did as he was told." She grabbed a handful of the coins and started to throw them at him.

"Don't," Slocum said.

"You are right. Why should I waste gold on the likes of him?" She spat on her brother. "Because of him, the gold was hidden away where we could not get it."

"We?"

She looked up sharply at Slocum, then laughed. It wasn't a pretty laugh.

"You do not think I permitted Denham to do anything to me I did not want? I planned the robbery, but Texas Rangers almost caught us. We ran, but *he* took the gold and hid it. Then he couldn't remember where. Or so he said." She kicked Don Rodrigo again.

"Stop that," Slocum said.

"What will you do, John? Shoot me in cold blood? He is my brother and after all I have done for him these long years, it is time to pay him back." She kicked Don Rodrigo again. This time the man whimpered like a whipped dog.

"You were tied up when I found you."

"Is it so hard to understand. I *like* such treatment. You are too gentle, John. I need a man who treats me roughly."

"So you and Denham's gang stole the gold, but Rodrigo hid it where you couldn't find it?"

"The Rangers came and we hid, but my brother drove away with the wagon. He could not remember what he did with it. Then he ran off before I could coax it from him."

"What about the cowboy in town?"

Consuela shrugged. "It was Luther's idea. Make those in Eagle Pass think Rodrigo killed, offer a reward, and they would scour the desert to find him. It was a stupid plan, but all the men in my life are stupid."

Slocum felt a coldness in his gut at the woman's words. She had used him to find her brother so she could worm the location of the gold from him. From Don Rodrigo's condition, she and Denham had not tortured him. Such a tactic probably would not have worked since El Loco's mind was lost to all rational thought. Somehow, they had gotten what they needed from him.

Then Consuela had shot her partner so she alone would claim the stolen gold.

"You were going to kill your own brother?"

She laughed harshly, giving Slocum all the answer he needed. Her blouse drooped down and fully exposed her breast. She made no move to cover herself because she saw she had his full attention.

"Why not? He is a burden I no longer can bear. He is a burden I no longer *want* to bear. But you, John, you are clever and good with a gun. We can go on from here. There is enough gold for the two of us to share."

"You're saying that only because I have the drop on you," he said. His grip steadied now as he learned what she actually was. The coyote and vultures out in the desert were more honest than Consuela de la Madrid y Garza.

"I would say it even if you put your pistol away," she said, and Slocum almost believed her. She was so appealing, with the sun shining down on her dark hair and turning it into something spectacular streaked with rainbows. Seldom had he seen a woman so lovely.

Slocum looked at El Loco, curled up in a tight ball on the ground at her feet, and knew the sort of woman she was.

"I've earned the gold," Slocum said.

"No!" Her rage flared and she reached for her rifle. Slocum cocked his six-shooter and froze her where she stood. She glared at him. "You cannot do this. Men died for this gold. Apaches chased us. Rangers almost caught us, and at least two posses hunt for him." She reared back as if she were going to kick her brother again.

Something about her action this time didn't seem right. Slocum jerked his head to one side as the barrel of a six-gun came crashing down from behind. His hat and the sudden move robbed the blow of its power, but Slocum was still knocked to his knees. He felt hands yanking his six-shooter from his grip, but he was too stunned to stop it.

"I wondered when you would show up," Consuela said. "Go on, lover. Kill him. Shoot him! Both of them!"

Through pain-clouded eyes Slocum saw Luther move around to the side of the wagon where he could look into the strongbox. The man had his six-gun drawn but pointed it at Consuela.

"I heard what you said to him. You'd go off with him, wouldn't you?"

"My love, no! It was all a ruse. I could do nothing while he held his six-shooter on me. You are the only one I love and want to be with."

"You double-crossed your own boss," Slocum accused. Luther spun on him, lifting his gun, but he did not fire.

"You don't know what a fool Denham was. He tried a dozen robberies and we never saw more than a few hundred dollars. Twice, *twice*, we tried to rob the Butterfield stage and you stopped us. He wasn't cut out to be a road agent. The only decent robbery we pulled was this." Luther gestured toward the wagon with its burden of gold.

Slocum tried to grab the outlaw's gun hand, but Luther stepped back so Slocum flopped into the dirt.

"You're pathetic," Luther said.

"Why don't you shoot him?" Consuela asked.

"I figure to make him die real slow. The way he was lookin' at you, I want him to suffer 'fore he gives up the ghost."

Slocum saw death coming. Consuela leveled her rifle and fired. Luther let out a tiny gasp before he died, disbelief on his face. He fell into the dust alongside Duke Denham.

"Now only one last detail is to be taken care of," Consuela said, moving to aim at Slocum. "I will be on my way."

He knew the next bullet from her rifle barrel would be for him. She had efficiently eliminated the last of the Duke Denham gang. It was Slocum's turn now.

"Good-bye, John. I can't say it was all pleasant, but a few moments were." She lifted her rifle, and then let out a cry of dismay as she toppled backward. Consuela hit the edge of the wagon, causing her rifle to rise and discharge into the air.

Slocum scrambled to his feet, but saw she recovered fast. Her brother had tackled her around the knees and brought her down unexpectedly, but she ignored the way Don Rodrigo held on to her and concentrated only on levering another round into the chamber and finishing Slocum off.

He grabbed for his six-gun in the dirt, but Consuela got off a round that sent it flying. He turned to grapple with her, but she struggled to jack in another round while kicking furiously at her brother, still intent on holding on to her legs. In a flash, Slocum estimated his chances and what would keep him alive. He dug his toes into the hard dirt and sprinted. The woman's next round missed him by feet. The one following tore through the air high above his head. Then he dodged into rocks and had only her curses being directed at him.

He pressed his back against a boulder and struggled to get his breath. His leg hurt like hell, and he knew he could not go much farther before it failed him. He touched the knife sheathed at his boot, but Consuela had a rifle and would never let him get close enough to use it. Throwing it was out of the question. Miss and he would be without any weapon at all.

"You won't get away from me, John," came her taunting words. "We spent some nice times together, but I will not let that stop me from shooting you. You were not that good a lover. I know. I have had many."

Slocum knew she was as likely to trigger off a round into his back as his front. Killing came easily to her. He realized he had been thinking with the wrong portion of his anatomy every second he had been with Consuela, but then she was very good at distracting men. Both Denham and Luther and their cooling bodies were mute testament to that.

"Come out, John, and let us be done. I will kill you quickly. I promise." He heard her shuffling along the rocky road. "You were a better lover than Luther. Does that please you?"

He looked around, and realized he had to reach his horse and the Winchester still riding in the saddle sheath. She was no fool and knew he would try. A big rock came easily into his hand. He judged distance and heaved it with all his strength, making it seem he had gone farther back down the road. Wasting no time, he limped away in the direction of his tethered mare.

"You won't get away, John. I gave you your chance to throw in with me."

She fired a few more times, but every slug went in the direction of the thrown rock. Slocum kept low, sometimes wiggling through the rocks on his belly like a snake, and finally reached his nervous horse. It would be easy enough to simply ride away and say to hell with the gold.

The way his leg threatened to give out under him at any instant made this a sensible thing to do. It was sensible, but Consuela had made him mad. She had pricked his vanity and played him for a fool. He would have ended up like Denham and Luther if it hadn't been for El Loco. Slocum felt he owed the crazy vaquero something, and all El Loco was likely to get from his sister was a bullet in the head.

Painfully dragging himself into the saddle, Slocum settled down and then drew his rifle. His mind turned over one scheme after another, but nothing that might work occurred to him. He was afraid that Consuela would try to use her hold over Don Rodrigo to force him into making a mistake.

Barely had that notion come to him than Slocum heard her call out, "I'll kill him. You like Rodrigo. If you don't show yourself, I'll kill him. His blood will be on your hands."

Slocum steeled himself to what he knew would follow. As Rodrigo cried out in pain at whatever torture Consuela meted out, Slocum turned his horse away. As good a marksman as Consuela was, Slocum was better. One shot and this would be over.

As he let the mare pick her way through the rocks, he felt rather than heard movement higher up the slope. He caught his breath as a shadow moved quickly and disappeared. Waiting a few minutes forced him to listen to Consuela's increasingly shrill demands for him to come to her so she could shoot him. Slocum finally caught sight of the Apache warrior silently advancing downhill on foot.

Where there was one brave there would be more.

Bereft of any real plan but knowing he had to act, Slocum let out a whoop and put his heels to the mare's flanks. He headed back downhill, away from Consuela and Don Rodrigo—and the gold. He had ridden only a few yards when he saw Apaches rising up all over the hillside above him. Swinging his rifle about, he fired a few rounds more to keep their attention than to kill. On horseback, galloping along, hitting anything would have been more luck than skill.

What he accomplished, though, saved both Don Rodrigo and his perfidious sister. The Apaches all rushed to get their horses and ride after Slocum. How far he could decoy them before they overtook him was rapidly becoming a worry. Why they all came after him rather than splitting up, half going after Consuela and the gold and the rest riding him down, was a mystery.

Leaning forward so his face pressed into the neck of his straining horse, Slocum heard Apache bullets singing through the air all around him. He rode as far as he could before he brought the horse to a trot to conserve its strength. The horse had endured as much as Slocum had since leaving Eagle Pass and had to be nigh on tuckered out, yet continued to respond when he asked it of her.

The war cries of the pursuing Apaches told him he had to find a spot to make a stand soon. Letting them box him in while they were on horseback meant his death. The only ace in the hole he had was that he knew his mare's capabilities. Apaches rode their horses till they fell dead under them.

Then they ate them, stole new horses, and repeated what for them was an endless cycle. That meant no brave hot on his heels knew how much more he could get out of his mount.

Slocum knew and appreciated his mare. He slowed, found a ravine, and cut down into it. The horse picked her way up the rocky arroyo as the Apaches passed by along the road. He'd had trouble tracking Denham earlier. Now the same hard, dry ground made it difficult for the Apaches to track *him*.

He worried that the arroyo was too deep and curved back toward the road in Consuela's direction. Slocum looked for a way out of the arroyo and away from the gold. Nature had cut this riverbed in such a way that he found himself back on the road, the Apaches far down the trail, and headed back in Consuela's direction.

He rested his horse as he considered what to do. Then his hand was forced. The Indians had finally realized he had given them the slip and were returning. A quick count from his vantage told him how difficult fighting them would be. There were only seven, but he was all alone. Seven Apaches against one injured man almost out of ammo. The odds weren't good at all for him.

Slocum did what he had to. He turned uphill and brought his horse to as fast a pace as she could tolerate. Apaches behind, Consuela ahead, he was caught in a vise that closed inexorably on him.

The war whoops of the Indians came closer. Then their bullets came closer still. One tore through Slocum's upper arm and burned like hell. He stayed low and retraced his path toward the buried wagon where Rodrigo stood running his fingers over the steel rim of one wheel.

Where Consuela had gone, he could not tell. The strong-box still rested in the back of the wagon, and the sunlight glinting off the gold told him the woman had not removed the loot.

Then he saw her making her way through the rocks, leading two horses. He doubted the second was for her brother, since Rodrigo never bothered looking up from where he stood by the wagon.

Consuela let out a howl of anger, dropped the reins, and lifted her rifle. Slocum bent low and raced past Don Rodrigo as Consuela fired. The bullet missed. He kept riding, knowing what this meant.

Within seconds, the Apaches thundered up the slope behind him and spotted Consuela. She took one final shot at Slocum and then trained her rifle on the Indians. This started the real firefight as all the Apaches opened fire on the woman, driving her back among the rocks.

Slocum kept riding until the sound of gunfire faded behind him.

18

Slocum slowed, and finally stopped his race away from the fight. He caught his breath as he listened to the ragged volleys telling how Consuela still fought. She had no chance against that many Apaches, and Slocum was torn about what he felt knowing that the cessation of gunfire meant she had died. He felt betrayed, but worse than this, he had been duped and hadn't known it until the woman leveled her rifle on him back at the freight wagon. She was a cold-blooded murderer and he had slept with her, never once guessing what she was capable of doing.

The way she treated her brother bothered him the most. Slocum knew that in times past the village idiots had been prized, but he had never found them especially worth bothering about. Something about Don Rodrigo touched him, though. The man came from wealth, and yet it did nothing to relieve the anguish he must feel when he went off on his wild flights of fancy. He owned the world, and none of it mattered to his crazed mind.

One minute, he could be reasonable. The next, he fancied himself a gunfighter or a matador or a singer. Slocum knew how irksome that could get, and didn't fault Consuela that much for wanting to be free of tending her brother's ever-shifting fantasies. What he found extremely distasteful was the way she chose to do it. She could have simply ridden away from Don Rodrigo and his hacienda, but had instead teamed up with Duke Denham and his gang. Not content with a life of plundering, she had double-crossed both Denham and Luther to get the gold from a robbery she had planned.

"It always comes back to Don Rodrigo," Slocum said sadly. He heard a frantic volley of shots, then silence. He knew Consuela must finally have succumbed to the Indians' attack, but what about her brother? Slocum didn't owe him squat, but El Loco was likable in a strange way.

Slocum wheeled his mare around and retraced his path, riding slowly as much to allow the horse to rest as to be sure he wasn't riding into the Apaches' guns. When he came to a spot where he might reveal himself to an Indian lookout, he dismounted, took his rifle, and made his way forward on foot. His leg throbbed constantly, and more than once collapsed under him. He caught himself and didn't make too much noise, but when rifles barked again, he fell flat to the ground, sure he had given himself away.

"You filthy savages!" The curse in Spanish following these words echoed down the canyon. Slocum wasn't too surprised that Consuela was still alive, but from the heavy return fire answering her challenge, she wouldn't be for long.

He moved more carefully until he lay like a sunning lizard atop a rock already boiling hot in the noonday sun. Ignoring the pain from the heat, he inched forward to get his first good look at the battleground. Consuela crouched under the rear of the half-excavated wagon. Above her in the wagon bed stood the strongbox, its lid closed to rob Slocum of the pleasure of the glittering contents.

Sprawled beside Consuela lay her brother. He might be dead for all the movement from him, but Slocum's keen eyes picked up small twitches to hint that Don Rodrigo was still among the living. Watching more carefully, he saw the man playing with a beetle, poking it with a stick and goosing it back and forth on the ground. He probably wasn't wounded, but only interested in bug racing.

Slocum slowly studied the terrain and saw no fewer than five Indians along the road, occasionally bobbing their heads up to draw fire. They knew Consuela had a limited amount of ammunition and wanted to exhaust her supply before attacking.

Or was it only a diversion? He studied the rocks above the woman, and saw another Apache working his way down silently. Slocum took aim and could have made an easy shot. Something stayed his hand—and saved his life.

In the rocks to his right rose the remaining Apache brave. If Slocum had fired, he would have alerted the warrior and been dead within seconds.

The five down the road got the signal, whooped, hollered, and revealed themselves all at once to gull Consuela into thinking they were attacking.

It worked. She stood to get a better shot, and the Indian in the rocks above plummeted down, knocking her to the ground. She rolled and got off a shot at her attacker. The Apache to Slocum's flank finished her with a single shot to the head. Consuela gasped and flopped forward, dead before her face burrowed into the bone-dry ground.

The other Apaches came running and jabbed her with their rifles. She did not stir, but Don Rodrigo did. The Indians jumped a foot when he sat up and began singing. Slocum considered how many Indian raiders he could cut down before they killed Don Rodrigo, but they just stared at him and made no effort to shoot.

"Hola, my good friends. Have you come to dance with me? Excellent!" Don Rodrigo began a weird, wild dance that kicked up dust that settled onto his dead sister. He never noticed as he cavorted and sang. Then he crouched down, facing away from Slocum, and began doing something in the dirt that remained hidden. But not to the Indians.

They all backed away and formed a tight circle, arguing about El Loco.

Slocum knew the Apaches feared crazies and would avoid them if possible. In Don Rodrigo's case, he had been dumped into their laps. Slocum worried that the war party might kill him and then ride on, but they stood at a respectful distance, arguing the matter. The war chief kept pointing in Rodrigo's direction, but the Mexican paid no notice. He was busy again poking a bug with a stick.

"Do come and see what this is, my good friends. Look. *Mira!*" Rodrigo sank to the ground and began lecturing them as if he knew all about bugs. He looked up and saw the Indians coming over.

Slocum held his breath. He didn't want Don Rodrigo to come to any harm, but he also didn't want to start a fight on the man's behalf that he could never finish. There had been bad blood between Duke Denham and the Indians from the way the war parties constantly dogged the outlaw's tracks, but that feud was over and done. The Apaches had won. Slocum might take out one or two of them, but they were warriors constantly on the alert for the cavalry. He had no chance of saving El Loco if the Indians decided to kill him.

But they didn't. They kept their distance as they ringed him, but not one made a move for knife or gun to kill him. Slocum slipped a bit farther back so he was less exposed as he spied on them.

"I am El Terrible!" The words rang loud and clear. Don Rodrigo began spinning a tale of how he had tamed all of West Texas after crossing the Rio Grande, then lurched into a story of robbing stagecoaches and banks and anyone who could reach high enough to the sky for him to steal their pokes. The Apaches murmured among themselves and began asking questions in broken English.

When they switched to Spanish, Slocum was less able to follow, but he perked up when he heard Don Rodrigo declare, "There are hundreds of soldiers on the way. I know this."

"How?" The war chief spat the word like a bullet.

El Loco tapped the side of his head and said, "I hear them inside. I know they will be here soon."

The Apaches exchanged looks, then began a heated discussion with the war chief, pointing up the canyon repeatedly.

"More blue coats than you can count. They come. I hear them!" Don Rodrigo tapped his ear and then nodded solemnly.

Slocum didn't need to be told what the Indians thought of this. They ran for their horses and vaulted onto them. In seconds, they were gone, heading for the Rio Grande to escape into Mexico. He was undecided whether to laugh or simply shoot Rodrigo to put him out of his misery. Heaving himself to his feet, Slocum made his way down the rock, stumbling and falling a couple times because of his game leg.

"Slocum, it is good to see you. My new friends just left."

"You told them the cavalry was on its way. There aren't soldiers within fifty miles of here." Slocum barely got the words out when he heard a distant trumpet followed by pounding hooves. Within minutes a guidon appeared and under it the soldier carrying it. In ten minutes, Slocum was surrounded by a company of anxious, eager buffalo soldiers.

The sergeant leaned down and said, "We been trackin' them red devils for a day now. You're damn lucky they kept on runnin'. You got any idea where they got off to?"

Before Slocum could say a word, Don Rodrigo piped up. "They have gone to Mexico. There is only one ford across the river they can use."

"You know it?"

"I know all! I am the finest frontiersman in all of Mexico!"

The sergeant looked at Slocum, who only nodded. Words failed him because the soldier was buying into El Loco's boasting just as the Apaches had.

"You show us?"

"I will do more than show you. I will lead you! I am a colonel in the *rurales*! Command is in my blood!"

"What about you, mister?" The sergeant fixed Slocum with a cold stare.

"I don't know what he's talking about. I saw the Apaches, but they lit out just before you rode up. They can't be more than a half hour ahead of you, but they were riding so hard they'd kill their horses under them."

"We got 'em then. They ain't gonna find new horses anywhere between here and the river. If they get into Mexico, now, that's another story."

"They can't get that far if you catch them on the Texas side of the border."

"We ain't 'lowed to cross the Rio Grande," the sergeant said. "Sound assembly. We're goin' after 'em right now."

The bugler spat out a few discordant notes as the soldiers formed a double file and waited for the command to advance.

"Señor," the sergeant said to Don Rodrigo, "get on your horse and let's ride."

"Adventure is before us," Rodrigo said, climbing into the saddle.

"Hold on, Don Rodrigo," Slocum said. He hurried to his horse and fetched the man's sombrero. Handing it up, he said, "You might need this to keep the sun off your head."

"A man can go plumb loco out here in the sun," the sergeant said.

Slocum tried not to laugh. Don Rodrigo solemnly fitted his sombrero down so the brim touched his ears, then adjusted the chin string with its fancy silver bead. He sat proudly on his horse, eyes ahead and looking for all the world like a rich hacienda owner.

He nodded once in acknowledgment to Slocum, and then rode off at the head of the column. The sergeant started his men, pausing only to say, "We'd help you bury the dead, mister, but we got to catch them what done this."

Slocum saw that the sergeant thought Denham and Luther had also been killed by the Apaches. That suited him just fine. No questions would be asked that he wasn't up to answering.

"I'll take care of them," he promised.

"Good man." With that, the sergeant trotted to the front of his men and started the troopers through the canyon on the Apaches' trail. Slocum watched them until the last soldier vanished from sight. Soon, even their dust had settled, leaving behind only deathly silence and stifling heat radiating off the canyon walls.

Slocum sat on a rock and looked at Denham, Luther, and Consuela. They deserved to be left where they lay as food for the coyotes and buzzards, but he couldn't do that. Consuela was Don Rodrigo's sister, even if he had ignored her when he rode off. For that, Slocum wouldn't have blamed a sane man after all the woman had done.

He stood, limped over, and picked up the shovel Don Rodrigo had used to unearth the wagon. Slocum began working, and ended up with a large grave dug that he rolled all three into. Another hour of work covered them up, and he piled rocks on top so the animals wouldn't dig. There was a reason cemeteries planted bodies six feet under. Animals couldn't smell the bodies at that depth. Slocum had to make do since the ground was so hard and rocky, but he doubted any of the three would care.

He threw down the shovel and went to the back of the wagon. The strongbox lid was closed. He knew that Consuela had had plenty of time to load it in the saddlebags on her horse, and that the horse had run off. Tracking a frightened horse in this terrain would be hard, but he would do it.

Slocum lifted the lid and stepped back in pleasant surprise. The gold was still in the box. He looked around guiltily, as if the cavalry troopers hadn't really chased after the Apaches and were waiting to catch him with the stolen gold.

He was alone. Alone with twenty thousand dollars in gold coins.

He licked dried, cracked lips and plunged his hand into the yellow metal coins to assure himself this was not some mirage. The hardness convinced him he wasn't hallucinating—and that he was a damn sight saner than Don Rodrigo de la Madrid y Garza. It took twenty minutes for him to transfer the gold to his saddlebags, and another ten to get on the trail leading downslope out of the canyon. Once he reached the desert, dotted with its sand dunes and creosote bush and mesquite, he wondered where he ought to head.

It didn't matter. He was rich now and could go anywhere to find interesting ways of spending his treasure. Slocum rode off whistling, and found it was easy to put Duke Denham, Consuela, and especially El Loco from his mind.

Watch for

SLOCUM AND THE LUCKY LADY

361st novel in the exciting SLOCUM series
from Jove

Coming in March!